AMIKOR ESIK A "VöRöS Hó"
WHEN THE "RED SNOW" FALLS

MY FIGHT WITH ANXIETY IN BUDAPEST

SIDAQ PRATAP SINGH

Made with ♥ on the Notion Press Platform
www.notionpress.com

I never thought of life as a race or a contest. Life has always felt like a massive colony full of playgrounds. Occasionally, I went to someone else's playground, and occasionally, someone came to mine. Budapest was one such playground where I met many outstanding individuals who supported and stood by me in my joys and sorrows. Budapest became a home away from home for me. This book is dedicated to everyone who was a part of my Budapest adventure.

Image courtesy: Niki Karagianni (website: nikikaragianni.pixieset.com)

Contents

Contents

Preface

The title is related to the Hungarian proverb "Majd ha piros hó esik! [ˈmɑjd ha piroʃ hoː ɛʃik] (When red snow falls!, When red snow will fall!) which is used for things that will never happen or are impossible to happen. The English equivalent is "When pigs fly!".

There was some discussion regarding the title.

Krisztina Bhagti Kaur (will tell about her in the second part) messaged me

> "*If you don't mind I would like to suggest a correction in the title. Even piros and vörös both means red, this term is used always with the word piros and we never say vörös hó. Amikor piros hó esik would be sound better in hungarian or Ha piros hó esik.*
>
> *Amikor and ha both means when in english, but there is a difference in their meanings. if you felt you were in a situation as if red snow felt, and you write about it, then use amikor, but if you were waiting for something that happens very rarely or never then use ha.*"

Then I asked Anna Szirmai (My therapist) about this and she replied

> "*I agree with your commentor here.*
>
> *I believed you used the term "voros" to refer to Hungary as a post-communist country, since we use this term to describe that era and the color of their symbols. The original expression indeed uses "piros". So if you didnt want to evoke political associations, I would use "piros" too. When it comes to "amikor" and "if" I would add another definition - although that of the commentator is precise in my opinion.*
>
> *Amikor - use this if something did happen.*
>
> *Ha - this means "if". Maybe use this if something didn't happen, but could have.*
>
> *Although I think using either would be understood the same way.*"

After this I did some research.

According to **Anna Wierzbicka,** in her article **The Semantics of colour: A new paradigm**

⁴⁴"In Hungarian, piros [...is] associated with blood inside the body, [...] whereas vörös is associated with blood spilled [...and] the fact that after a while, blood spilled tends to get darker could explain the inclusion of darker shades in vörös."[2] Common collocations include piros lap (red card in football), piros rózsa (red rose) and piros tojás (red egg, given by a girl to a boy during Easter)

- *Wierzbicka, Anna (2006). "The semantics of colour: A new paradigm". Progress in Colour Studies: Volume I. Language and culture. John Benjamins Publishing Company: 11–12. ISBN 9027232393*

In the Paper **"The Hungarian colour terms piros and vörös A corpus and cognitive linguistic account",Réka Benczes** and **Erzsébet Tóth-Czifra** came up with three hypotheses

⁴⁴1. as vörös had more time to undergo idiomatization, there will be significant differences and systematic trends between the type/token ratios of the two terms

2. piros is a more generic term used for a larger and looser range of concepts, while vörös is associated with a more limited range of concepts, and

3. piros is mostly used in its primary, literal sense, while vörös is more inclined to be used in a figurative sense.

- *Benczes, Réka; Tóth-Czifra, Erzsébet (June 2014). "The Hungarian colour terms piros and voros A corpus and cognitive linguistic account". Acta Linguistica Hungarica. 61 (2): 123–152. doi:10.1556/ALing.61.2014.2.1*

In his Book **"Language and Nationality: Social Inferences, Cultural Differences, and Linguistic Misconceptions", Pietro Bortone** writes,

*⁴⁴Hungarians see [dark and light variants of Red] as either **piros and vörös,** which they concieve as two different basic colours . To*

*Hungarian speakers neither can subsume the other. Hungarian **piros and vörös** thus not fully translated by "**Red**" and, ultimately by "**Dark Red**" and "**Bright Red**" because such translations would fail to convey the neat distinction that Hungarians make: **piros and vörös** are concieved as two unrelated colours. Indeed **piros and vörös** have each also distinct connotations, associations and metaphorical uses .....*

- *Bortone, Pietro (23 September 2021). Language and Nationality: Social Inferences, Cultural Differences, and Linguistic Misconceptions. Bloomsbury Publishing. pp. 70–71. ISBN 9781350071667*

After reading all this I decided to stick with this title as the word **vörös** triggers a reaction that is very interesting to listen to or read. I have intentionally kept the Hungarian alphabet capital in the title plus the sentence structure is in a way that it might like a little amateurish or "Google translated" to Hungarian readers.

There is also an alternate Hungarian title for each chapter. I got the idea from the Indian film "Sir" released in 2019, whose Hungarian title was "Tû, cérna, szerelem (Needle, thread, love)".

- *Gera, Rohena (Writer, director) (20 September 2018). Sir (Motion Picture) (in Hindi and English). India*

Hungarian Poster

"Tillotama Shome shared my Instagram Story. For her performance in the film, she won the Filmfare Award for Best Actress (Critics)."

Foreword

Sidaq was my student at the Budapest Metropolitan University, learning about the Psychology of Art
for a semester while completing his BA education in Film. We started our psychological counseling
work in January of 2021., when he returned home from Budapest. During our approx. 50 sessions
overarching 3 years, we always met online.

Our process always focused on working with the issues and emotions arising in the here and now,
but we covered major lifetime events associated with his current state.
His original challenges with building human connections arose from his childhood trauma at the age of 8
years old, when a sudden onset of epilepsy impaired his vision and resulted in a lengthy period of recovery.
After this event, his peers bullied him repeatedly, which made him withdraw into his own world, unable to
build friendships.

Due to the above, movies always played a major role in his life. They served as a means to communicate his
inner life to others and build connections. Studying film in Budapest was a major step towards achieving his life's goal to work with movies. However, his 2-year-long stay in Budapest has proven to be very meaningful in both positive and negative ways. He connected to the city and some of his schoolmates deeply. However, he also experienced bullying and racism, both on the streets, at work, from his employer, and at school from his teachers. This trauma caused him to give up on his life goal, withdraw completely, strengthened his depression and pushed him to the edge of suicide. Thankfully, his life was spared, and he decided to move back to his hometown.

During our work, I have gotten to know Sidaq as a person with a deep and rich inner life, much of
which is not shared with anyone. He has a supportive familial background, and some friendships kept alive
online.

He communicates in writing much easier than in real-time or in person. He connects the living world to
nature with ease and finds comfort and lessons to learn from them. Also, his travels are like medicine
because there he is pushed to reach out and connect to people and the culture around him - he always
returns feeling more alive, but being home deflates his motivation and energy to act over and over again.
He is more visible in these more distant, visual fields of life, and one can get to know his authentic self.
Whereas at home, he is afraid to open up, because he feels lacking in social skills and wants to avoid
hurting others with his messages. However, during therapy, I have only experienced his humor,
attentiveness, and respect - even when giving me some negative feedback or sharing difficult issues. He
has never hurt or burdened me, and I am thankful that he shares his insights about the world.

Anna Szirmai

Budapest, 2nd April, 2024.

"Anna Linda Szirmai, is a psychologist working as an organizational developer, individual- and group therapist in Budapest, Hungary for the last 15 years. During her therapeutical work she apply the thoughts and techniques of Client-Centered Therapy and Psychodrama."

ਜਦੋਂ "ਲਾਲ ਬਰਫ਼" ਡਿਗਦੀ ਹੈ

(Translation of title in Gurmukhi script of Panjabi)

جدوں "لال برف" ڈِگدی ہے

(Shahmukhi script of Panjabi)

Jadõ "lāl baraf" ḍigadī hai

(Latin script of Panjabi)

"ᏌᎡ ᎥᏦᎻᏦᎷ" Ꮡ ᎤᏔᎥᎦ ᎻᎠᎤᏔᏓᏑ

Title in Hungarian runes

Hungary follows the **Eastern name system**, meaning the conventional name order is "surname first, followed by the given name." As an example:

Kovács is a surname from Hungary.

János is his given name.

As a result, in Hungary, the complete name would be "Kovács János."

This book uses Western name order when mentioning Hungarian individuals.

Content Warning: *This book contains depictions and discussions of racism, self-harm, suicide, and various forms of violence.*

PART - I

Anxiety and indiánság

*Note: The title references the essay **"The Anxiety of Indianness: Our Novels in English" by** Meenakshi Mukherjee.*

- Mukharjee, Meenakshi (27 November 1993). "The Anxiety of Indianness: Our Novels in English". Economic and Political Weekly. 28 (48): 2607–2611.

**indiánság [ˈindijaːnʃaːg] = Indianness*

CHAPTER ONE

HUNGARY AND CINEMA

Hungarian title: Szívből

Translation: "From the Heart"

Note: Hungarian title is a reference to the 1999 Hindi language film "Hum Dil De Chuke Sanam (I have given my heart away, darling, released internationally as Straight From the Heart)." The film tells the story of a newlywed man (Vanraj) who learns that his wife (Nandini) is in love with another man (Sameer) and decides to bring them together. Vanraj and Nandini travel to Italy to find Sameer. The interesting thing about this film is that it was shot in Budapest, which the makers passed off as Italy to viewers. In the end, Vanraj eventually reunites them and bids Nandini goodbye before walking away. She apologises to Sameer and tells him that she loves Vanraj. She races down a bridge to reunite with Vanraj, and the best part is that it is the Chain Bridge in Budapest.

- *Sanjay Leela Bhansali (director) (18 June 1999). Hum Dil De Chuke Sanam [I have given my heart away, darling] (Motion picture) (in Hindi). India: Bhansali Productions. OCLC 745429647*

2.39 :1

Interview

In August 2018, I went to the Hungarian Embassy in New Delhi for my visa interview. As we Punjabis don't have a good reputation in the Hungarian Embassy (Punjabis use Hungary as the gateway to the Schengen zone, and after staying for a few months in Hungary, they disappear), Ms. **Beáta Fal**, who was taking my interview, gave a reaction like she was thinking "Oh God another one" but when I started speaking, her body language changed and we talked about various topics. She then asked me the meaning of my name as she had heard this name for the first time in her life. After that, she saw my mother's name, and She was surprised to know that a Sikh lady has the name "Sophia" so I told her the story that my Nani (maternal grandmother) used to read Russian novels in Hindi and from there, my mother got her name. She was so excited to hear that and said "Then she will also read Hungarian books in Hindi as well" and she left the room to give me some Hungarian books translated into Hindi. She could not find a novel so she gave me a slip with recommendations and some booklets about Hungary and Hungarian history which she could collect in that short period. Ultimately, she said, "It was lovely talking to you. I hope you get a good wife in the future, an intelligent one". I still have no idea how that was related but overall it was a wonderful experience.

"

> *Sidaq = Faith, belief, trust, truth, contentment, patience*
> *From Arabic "ṣidq ", "truth, sincerity"*
> "

4

slip with recommendations and booklets given by Ms. Beáta Fal

In 2018, I went to Budapest to study filmmaking.

1.66:1

2018 Nov 13

Two Great things about Hungary and Hungarians are that there are lots of venues showcasing all World Cinema and that Natives give all due Respect by being seated until the credits are over. This is what Cinema deserves. Thank you Puskin Art Mozi Toldi mozi and Művész Art Mozi.

Toldi Mozi

"Address book;
   Toldi Mozi, Budapest, Bajcsy-Zsilinszky út 36-38, 1054 Hungary
   Puskin Mozi, Budapest, Kossuth Lajos u. 18, 1053 Hungary
   Művész Art Mozi, Budapest, Teréz krt. 30, 1066 Hungary"

Beginning

My first class was with **Dr. Katalin Aknai,** who used to give us tours of Budapest. An art historian by profession, she showed us many historical sites and the best bakeries in Budapest. Another exciting thing is that at the same time, the Prime Minister of Turkey, Recep Tayyip Erdoğan, came to Hungary on an official visit. You could see security everywhere and a sniper standing on every other building.

My second class was film editing with **Gábor Kertai.** The first challenge I had at university was comprehending the Hungarian keyboard, which differs from the standard QWERTY keyboard in various ways, like the position of the Y and Z keys being swapped on the Hungarian keyboard.

Ticket

Hungarian title: Havi Budapest-bérlet felsőoktatásban tanulóknak

"Translation: "Monthly Budapest pass for students in higher education""

Monthly and Quarterly Transport Passes

1.66:1

My Monthly/Quarterly Budapest pass from 9 October 2018 to 6 April 2021.
Thousands of stories are buried in each pass.
My favorite excuse after getting late was, "Metro was not working, So I had to take a replacement bus."

*"The Budapest Metro M3 (Blue Metro) has been under repair for many years and passengers have to take the "M3 Replacement Bus." The reconstruction work of the metro began on 6 November 2017, with the closure of all stations between the southern terminal Kbánya-Kispest and Nagyvárad tér station. According to **Daily News Hungary,** "Replacement buses run at very high frequencies, more than 1 minute during peak periods, and more than 100 articulated, accessible, air-conditioned buses are used." According to the Official website of the reconstruction project of metro line M3, "On 22 May 2023, the entire metro line M3 and all stations will be opened to passenger traffic" (a day before my birthday)"*

CHAPTER TWO

ROMA VAGY INDIAI [ROMA OR INDIAN]

1.78:1

In November 2018, I went to withdraw money from an ATM at night. As soon as I put the card in the machine, two policemen started coming toward me and one of them tapped me hard on the shoulder. They started shouting at me in Hungarian. When they calmed down a bit, I told them that I couldn't speak Hungarian, and after hearing this, they asked me for a passport or any other ID, I was not carrying any ID, so they went with me to my building and after checking my ID, they left the building.

A few days later I went shopping in a grocery store, I was picking up items from the shelf in the store and a security guard came towards me and started speaking in Hungarian. I was confused again about what was going on. He then spoke in English and said that he wanted to check my bag. He checked my bag, said thank you, and left. Later, a Hungarian who saw what happened told me that the guard thought I was a "Roma thief" (words used by that guard in Hungarian). From that day I used to get ready to go to the grocery store as if I am going to someone's wedding.

The following day, I was standing at the Astoria metro station when a Hungarian approached me furiously and began yelling, threatening to strike me. I fled that location and proceeded to a neighbouring restaurant to conceal. Sameman approached me and began apologising. He claimed to have fought with a Roma man on the subway and was hunting for him. He thought I was that person. He even expressed regret for uttering racist insults.

Hungary has a sizable Roma community, which is one of the country's major ethnic minority groups. Roma, also known as Romani or Gypsies, have their own culture, language, and history. According to various analysts and Romani organisations, Hungary's Roma population spans between 500,000 and 800,000 individuals, making it one of Europe's largest Roma communities; However, in the 2011 census, only 315,583 people are registered as Romani. The term "Gypsy" is considered derogatory by many members of the Romani community,

The Roma community has a complex and diverse origin. They are believed to have originated from the Northern and northwestern Indian regions of Rajasthan and Punjab. I am also from the same region, the reason for all the confusion.

According to Milena Hübschmannová, "While the Romani lexicon is closer to Hindi, Marwari, Punjabi, etc., in the grammatical sphere we find many similarities with the East Indian language, Bengali."

Antiziganism and The "Gypsy Crime" narrative

"The 2008–2009 neo-Nazi murders of Roma in Hungary were a series of racially motivated attacks that targeted the Roma community in Hungary. Over a span of about a year, between 2008 and 2009, a group of far-right extremists carried out a series of violent assaults and murders against Roma individuals."

Antiziganism, or negative prejudice, is a deeply established societal issue in Hungary, resulting in Romani minority marginalization, social exclusion, and human rights abuses. Despite their contributions to Hungarian culture, Romani communities have endured institutional oppression. Factors such as financial disparities, cultural differences, and the reinforcing of negative stereotypes have exacerbated this prejudice.

Antiziganism manifests itself in a multitude of forms in Hungary, perpetuating a cycle of prejudice and discrimination. Stereotypes of Romani people as criminals, lazy, and untrustworthy are widespread, influencing public opinion and exacerbating societal divides. Images in the media and political discourse regularly reinforce these stereotypes, creating a hostile environment for the Romani minority.

Another type of antiziganism is spatial segregation. Romani villages, usually lack basic infrastructure, adequate housing, and access to essential services such as education and healthcare. This separation promotes poverty and marginalization, preventing Romani from advancing economically. Antiziganism goes beyond prejudice and discrimination to violent attacks and hate crimes against the Romani community. Over the years, there have been several incidents of racially motivated attacks, arson, and even murders against Romani individuals and groups. The absence of effective legal instruments to prevent hate crimes, as well as the inability to hold perpetrators accountable, has created a climate of fear and insecurity among the Romani population.

"Gypsy Crime" is a contentious and problematic narrative that stigmatizes and criminalizes the Romani people. The tale of "Gipsy Crime" perpetuates stereotypes and biases against Romani people, portraying them as fundamentally criminal and involved in various illegal activities like as theft, fraud, and organized crime. Misinformation, cultural misconceptions, and historical prejudices typically feed this narrative.

"More than 700 members of far-right organisations descended on the western Hungary town of Devecser in August 2012. The demonstrators made their way to a street where they thought there were Roma families after conducting their protest in the village's centre. They were chanting "Gypsy criminals …We will set your homes on fire … You will burn inside your houses!" (Translated from Hungarian)"

International Roma Day

"My post on Instagram on the occasion of International Roma Day 2021

- *Singh, Sidaq Pratap [@zindagikhudbkhud] (8 April 2021). "April 8 is recognised as #internationalromaniday" – via Instagram.*

April 8 is recognized as **International Romani Day**
A day to celebrate Romani culture and raise awareness of the issues facing Romani people. I met a large community living in Hungary. Around 450,000 to 1 million Romani people live in Hungary.

Here, I tried to compare the Romani Language, a western Indo-Aryan Language spoken by Romani people all around the world (not Romanian; many people confuse it with this romance language), with my mother tongue, Panjabi, a northwestern Indo-Aryan Language, as I have seen linguists compare these two Languages a lot.

I was able to communicate with one Romani-speaking food delivery guy using common words like "Thal'ay," a word for down, while I was instructing him to put the food down near the door during a contactless delivery. Other than that, over the years, both Languages have changed due to the influence of Balkan and other languages on Romani and Perso-Arabic influence on Punjabi.

Romani and Punjabi

15

Flag (above), Hungarian variant (below)

Flag of the Romani people and Hungarian variation.It was adopted in 1971 and 1978, at the first and second World Romani Congresses (WRC), it was endorsed by representatives of various Romani communities. The flag has a background of blue and green, which stand in for the heavens and the earth, respectively. A 16-spoke red dharma chakra, or cartwheel, is in the middle of the flag.

Hungarian Romas use a variant flag with an Eight-spoked wheel.

Weer Rajendra Rishi

Weer Rajendra Rishi (1917–2002) was an Indian linguist, diplomatic translator, and Romani studies scholar. He was born Waliati Ram Rishi in Makarampur, Jalandhar District (now Shaheed Bhagat Singh District), Punjab on 23 September 1917.

Rishi pioneered the study of Romani language and culture in India. He authored several books on the subject, including "Romani-Punjabi-English Conversation" (1980) "Roma: The Panjabi Emigrants in Europe, Central and Middle Asia, the USSR, and the Americas" (1983), and "The Romani Language: A Linguistic Introduction" (1993). He was also a strong advocate for the rights of the Roma people. Rishi was the Director of the Indian Institute of Romani Studies at Chandigarh and the editor of "Roma - Half-Yearly Journal on the Life, Language and Culture of Roma."

Hungarian, Panjabi, and Romani

"Hungarian and Panjabi
English: Dog
Hungarian: kutya (ˈkucɒ)
*Panjabi: kuttā (from Ashokan Prakrit *????? *kutta)*
English: One thousand
Hungarian: ezer (Iranian borrowing, possibly from Alani)
Panjabi: Hazār (from Persian hazâr)
*Both are ultimately from Proto-Indo-Iranian *sajʰásram, from Proto-Indo-European *ǵʰéslom.*
English: Stink, Bad smell

Hungarian: bűz (Iranian borrowing)

Panjabi: Bu (from Persian بو bu)

English: Flesh, Meat

Hungarian: hús (Iranian borrowing)

Panjabi: Goshat (from Persian gušt)

Hungarian: tinó = Steer (From Oghur, ultimately of Iranian origin)

Punjabi: Dhenu (Tenu) – Cow, Milch cow (from Sanskrit धेनु dhenú)

Hungarian: vidék = country, countryside

Panjabi: Vidēsh = Foreign, abroad, Overseas (from Sanskrit वदिश videś)

Hungarian: duttyán = Food stall, Booth (from Ottoman Turkish دکان dükkân, from Arabic dukkān, "shop")

Panjabi: Dukān = Shop, Store (from Persian dokkân, from Arabic dukkān)

English: Valley

Hungarian: Vádi

Panjabi: Vādī/Wādī

Both are from From Arabic wādī, "valley"

English: Pocket

Hungarian: Zseb (from Ottoman Turkish ceb, cep)

Panjabi: Jēb (from Persian jeyb)

Both are ultimately from Arabic jayb, "pocket")

Hungarian: kéró = (slang) Pad (From Romani kher "house", from Sanskrit गृह gṛhá, "house, home")

Punjabi: Garahi= House, Dwelling (from Sanskrit गृह gṛhá, "house, home")

Hungarian: Manus = (colloquial) guy, man, bloke (Borrowed from Romani manuś, from Sanskrit manuṣya, "man")

Panjabi: Manukkh (From Sanskrit manuṣya)

Hungarian: Csór = (transitive, slang) To steal (from Romani ćor, from Sanskrit cora "thief")

Panjabi: Chor = Thief (from Sanskrit cora)

Hungarian: Csóró = (slang) poor (from Romani ćorro "poor", from Sanskrit chora)

Panjabi: (Western dialects) Chōrā = Orphan (from Sanskrit chora)

Hungarian: séró = (slang) Head, Hair, Haircut (from Romani śero "head", from Sanskrit śiras)

Panjabi: Sir (from Sauraseni Prakrit: ??? sira, from Sanskrit śiras)

*Both are ultimately from Proto-Indo-Aryan *śŕHas, from Proto-Indo-Iranian *ćŕHas, from Proto-Indo-European *ḱŕh₂ -os, from *ḱerh₂ - ("head")*

Hungarian: kaját = (slang) to eat (from Romani khal, from Sauraseni Prakrit ???? khādi, from Sanskrit khādati)

Panjabi: Khāṇā = to eat (from Sauraseni Prakrit ???? khādi, from Sanskrit khādati)

Other languages

Hungarian: csávó = (slang) Boy, Man (Borrowed from Romani ćhavo "boy", from Sauraseni Prakrit chāva, "baby animal")

Marathi: chāvā = Cub, (slang) boyfriend (from Sauraseni Prakrit chāva, "baby animal")

Hungarian: pia/piál = (slang) to booze (from Romani pijel "he drinks")

Hindi: Piyā = Drank (From Sanskrit pī "to drink" + yā "attained")"

CHAPTER THREE

DALAI LAMA, EUROPEAN TRADITION AND INDIAN STYLE

Hungarian title: Indiai gyökerek, magyar hagyományok

Translation: "Indian roots, Hungarian traditions"

Note: Hungarian title is a reference to the interview of George Szirtes, titled "Magyar gyökerek, angol hagyományok (Hungarian Roots, English Traditions)"

- *"Magyar gyökerek, angol hagyományok" [Hungarian Roots, English Traditions] (in Hungarian). 14 September 2001. Budapest: Élet és Irodalom. Vol. 45, no. 41.*
- *"Hungarian Roots, English Traditions" (in English). The Hungarian Quarterly. 42 (164): 100–106. September 2001. ISSN 1217-2545.*

Good man dī lālṭain
Bad man dā dīvā
One two three India will be free

"A Pinglish (Punjabi + English) slogan used by Punjabis during the Colonial era. It means "Good men Britishers brought the lantern with them but we Bad men Indians are happy with our Diya lamp, Soon India will be free"."

In October 2019, I received an email from my screenwriting teacher:

"Dear Sadiq, I know you came late in the first semester -- but were you in class when we discussed the scripts for Hotel Chevalier, James, etc? It gives you the basic format of how to write a film, how to think in situations and create scenes. That is what I have been trying to teach for a year now.

Here az METU all your professors work in the European (or Western) tradition, we have no experience in Indian filmmaking, if you want to work according to the Indian tradition, you should find an film school in India.

Please write a synopsis (max 1 page) for next class that can be used as a story for a 4-5 minute film.

If you have any complaints about the school, please send a formal letter to the school, or to the people concerned, I cannot help you solve problems beyond my class."

Other than he wrote my name wrong (Even when I corrected him in the next emails, he was writing Sadiq, I think he was mocking me), my major problem with the email was the line "Here az METU all your professors work in the European (or Western) tradition, we have no experience in Indian filmmaking if you want to work according to the Indian tradition, you should find an film school in India." So I asked him what nonsense is this (in a formal way) to which his reply was, "Every time I explain what the task is, you say you do it the Indian way, that is what you said yesterday, that the writing you submitted was written in the Indian tradition, that you write in the Indian tradition. I do not know what the Indian tradition for screenwriting is, and it is not what I give out as tasks. Please try to let go and think in scenes and situations for your short film. Thank you." which was a lie I never talked about Indian cinema, writing or filmmaking being different even once. Even I said something else, and he misunderstood it. Later on I realized it was not my fault it is something that he has created in his mind after watching 3 to 4 Satyajit Ray Films and few Bollywood films. In every class, he was like you people from here are like this, and people from there people are like that. Whenever I used to ask him something his reply was always "Maybe in India you people....." and in the email, he says that I always talk about India". He is basically a person who creates a world on third-party sources for eg. In one class he was asking Turkish students that is "Mustang (a Turkish film released in 2015) authentic as his Turkish filmmaker friend once told him that the woman who directed that film grew up in France and the film is not real. To which the Turkish students replied it was realistic. From here you can get an Idea about his knowledge of different cultures. In another class (I was not present there it was narrated by a friend), which was divided into two groups one group was of female students and the other was of males. So one day one boy from the second group came early he saw him and said "Hey did you notice one group consists of only boys and others only girls, Is there something written in the Quran about this looking at the hijab-wearing girls sitting in front. It was not the first time he cracked a joke like this it was like his idiotic way of telling people that he knows a lot of things, etc.

Let's return to the email. The second thing which was problematic for me was his statement, "If you have any complaints about the school, please send a formal letter to the school, or to the people concerned, I cannot help you solve problems beyond my class." I never asked him for any kind of help I once complained about the position of TV in his classroom as it was difficult to watch anything to which he replied "write an email to uni it's not my problem."

After I complained about the "Indian style" line, he replied, "Than I must have misunderstood you, you were talking about not writing the way I expect because you write according to different rules." Only he knows about those rules. After which I replied:

Dear Mr. ####

I think I will not be able to attend your classes anymore as I think my mental health is more important than the grade

1) Indian system is similar to other systems I don't know where you have read or heard that it is different. If you say I said something like than I don't think you ever understood a word I ever said in your class

2) I know whom to approach if I have any issues. I have always approached the concerned teacher if I had any problems with then or used the feedback form or Sic for other university related issues . I never discussed anything with you which was not related to your class. So I don't know what was the meaning of last line. The only thing I remember is about the TV screen in M305 as it was difficult to see it from back for which you replied it's not your business.

3) I explained the reason of using large font in the second class but still you made fun of it class twice after that including last class. (I have a scar in my right eye Cornea and because of that I am almost blind in that eye. I explained to him that this is the reason I write in the large font but he made fun of this twice in class)

4) You should talk only about your class only you don't even know what is happening in other classes so how can you that I want to work in Indian system in other classes (Reply here we teachers work in European style)

5) Out of all classes I attended in 3 semester Monday's class was the only class I used the word "Indian" and you developed a whole conspiracy theory about it which is not at all acceptable including your insensitive "Go back to your country" remark (I twisted your words here as you did with the Indian thing).

6) I had mailed the issue to HOD to know if there is any solution to this
I don't think I can gain any knowledge from your class as my words are being turned and twisted into something else and it's effecting my mental health which is more important than getting a degree or grade "

His reply to this was next level "Obviously, I have nothing against India or Asian culture, Satyajit Ray is one of my favourire film directors. I have been a member of a Buddhist community for 8 years, and for years I used to meet the Sangha every week and go on Buddhist retreats every summer. I have read many books by the Dalai Lama who is the religious leader closest to me in the world. I am also a huge fan of Korean, Japanese, Chinese and Iranian cinema, but obviously, that is to the North and West. Let's sit down with Diana and see how we can make it work. I am not trying to offend or hurt you in any way, I am trying to teach you and asking you not to do it in a different way, in a different trasition with different rules"

I have observed this pattern in various "Intellectuals" like him, who try to defend their actions by telling how they have long association with the culture you belong to. The lesson I learned from this is that in the future there might be a time when I will say something culturally insensitive because of my ignorance or stupidity. I will never try to defend my actions like he is trying to defend his by taking the names of Dalai Lama and Satyajit Ray.

After this email, I lost my patience and replied " I was just talking about the hypothetical traditions you created based on 9 classes I attended. Your argument is just like a molester who is saying he has a daughter at home after molesting someone. You were talking about ray. You know he was an illustrator so he used to draw the whole story before writing the screenplay and that is not Indian style.

P.S. My biggest regret is I started hating the whole city because of this one Bad fish in the pond but later I realized that even though he claims to be various things, in reality, he is the cheapest example of all. If you want to meet better people from his profession or community you need to explore the city. He is like that cheap Global franchise burger who is easily available that's why you will see him everywhere talking about equality or Inclusion which makes me laugh.

George Szirtes (1948–) is a Hungarian-born British poet and translator. He was born in Budapest on 29 November 1948, and emigrated to the United Kingdom during the 1956 Hungarian Uprising. He is notable for translating Hungarian literature into English. Szirtes has made substantial contributions to the literary scene, blending his Hungarian roots with his experiences in the United Kingdom.

CHAPTER FOUR

TURUL TURMOIL

Hungarian title: Nagy cápa, aki egy kis halra vadászik

"Translation: A big shark hunting a small fish
    Note: Hungarian title is a reference to Turul's 2005 Netlog
"Cápavadászat kishalaknak (londoni napló 2.)" [Shark hunting for
small fish (London Diary 2.)]

- "Cápavadászat kishalaknak (londoni napló 2.)" [Shark hunting
  for small fish (London Diary 2.)]. Litera – az irodalmi portál (in
  Hungarian). London: Litera.hu. 1 November 2005.

1.37:1

Paṛh Paṛh Ālim Fāzil Hō'i'ā
Kadē Āpṇē Āp Nū Paṛhi'ā na'ī
Jā Jā Vaṛdā Mandar Masītā
Kadē Man Āpṇē Vich Vaṛi'ā na'ī
You studied and became knowledgeable
But you never studied yourself
You go again and again to mosques and temples*
But you never explored your own self
– Baba Bulleh Shah (Panjabi philosopher and poet, 1680–1757)

"

*Here, Mosques and temples are the libraries that Turul visits."

So I went to the HOD, and he (the teacher) was not there; only the HOD was sitting there, and they said it's the first time it's happening here (well actually, the first time someone complained about it), and they were not prepared for this kind of situation, so they gave me an option. The subject was divided into two parts: screenwriting and direction, one part taken by this Great personality and the other by another teacher (she was more horrible, Roger Ebert tried to whitewash her image in his book "Roger Ebert's Movie Yearbook 2003" but she is nothing like what is mentioned in the book) so I just need to attend the direction class.

The same day, I received a message on Facebook:

"Dear Sidaq,

The world is a beautifully diverse place. In Film History, we talk about different traditions. There is Hollywood Cinema, French and British and Eastern European cinema, there is Japanese and Korean and Iranian and Indian cinema, among many other traditions. These terms are not based on ethnicity, but on culture and region --- and they are internationally accepted and used. Every tradition has great filmmakers and films. Every tradition is equally special and unique in its own ways. We must cherish and celebrate the diversity of traditions. In class, you said you are not doing the task I gave you because you work in a different tradition. In my knowledge filmmakers start by writing a synopsis, that is a few paragraphs about the basic concept, the storyline, the characters. That is the way I know it and the way I teach it --- I am still not sure what you meant by working in a different tradition. I think it is all based on a misunderstanding, however, it got out of hand. You wanted to be with #### (direction teacher) and avoid my class, your wish was granted. I think we should close the dispute here. I do think you have been unfair in your judgement, but let's move on and focus on our work, I have altogether 50 students to teach, and you have several films to shoot. Let's focus on these tasks ahead of us. I wish you good luck with your work. Best

"

I replied:

Thank you so much for writing my name correctly. I never used the word "tradition" or any other synonym to it in class. I never said I wanted to avoid your class I reported your email and they said this is the only option as there is only one writing teacher in university. I have requested the same for 10 December presentation because I want unbiased and unprejudiced people present during my presentation. You skipped the "email part" (which was the main problem) in the story you narrated to other teacher and maybe also to HOD, it was more about my mentality, my behaviour and my problems with university and I don't trust you after hearing that version. I discussed this matter with few senior students as well and none of them tried to defend you at all they were like *Turul says a lot of things like this So maybe I am not the only who has to work on his ways (I never used these stories or incidents as a weapon against you in any of my complaints. I just wrote about your behaviour towards me) Thank you so much I learned a lot about humanity from you Warm Regards Sidaq (The guy you think does not belong here)

1)Dear Mr *Turul your basic argument was that Indians use different traditional methods to make film. Well the format of screenplay, terminology, shot division, camera angles, Action and cut are same everywhere only the activities between the action and cut might be different for some people but that is interpretative (I will try to write it in second part)

2) Talking about cultural diversity I come from a country where after every few kilometers the dialect changes and few more kilometers people speak a totally different language. Even if you talk about my language it is the written in two totally different scripts (Gurmukhi in India and Shahmukhi in Pakistan) yet we live together as one community as we believe in unity in diversity same thing goes for Cinema in India. We produce a lot of films in more than 22 languages and some states even produce bilingual/multilingual films, They are made by people from different states speaking different languages , following different religions etc . That's Indian cinema but there are different "international" terms for Indian cinema like European, American, Nigerian etc and they are not 100% correct as they have just seen one galaxy of this big universe and that becomes the part of discrimination when we talk about cinema. Indian cinema is not just bollywood there are a lot of woods to explore here. You cannot justify things by using " international" everywhere. Your behavior is called "Intellectual racism" where a person thinks he knows a lot about a different culture through reading literature, watching movies and in your case your experiences with your students. As I said before I have no issues with other things that were written in the mail as I know where I am struggling . But I definitely have an issue with this line " Here az METU all your professors work in the European (or Western) tradition, we have no experience in Indian filmmaking, if you want to work according to the

Indian tradition, you should find an film school in India. " This line was racist and insensitive and not at all acceptable and it contradicts everything you wrote above about diversity and cultural tolerance . I wish you were the same person you claimed in this interview.

I identify myself as European and very cosmopolitan. When it comes to ancestry my heritage is mixed: beside Hungarian lineage I have ancestors of German, Ruthenian, Slovak, and Polish origin – typical for people of the ex-Habsburg Monarchy. Even though I do not speak any of these languages, I am proud of my colourful national background.

- From Turul's 2013 interview. "

P.S Please don't use our pride Ray as a tool of discrimination

*"*I changed his name to "Turul [ˈturul]", a mythological bird of prey. I once replied to him that you are that Saker falcon who thinks he is the legendary Turul. (Can't find that email now)."*

Sometimes, I think it is my fault only once I told him the story of how in India, occasionally we have different dialogue writers because people speak various languages. I gave an example of a Bengali filmmaker who was going to direct a Hindi language film and he wrote his screenplay in English which was later translated in Hindi and a separate writer was hired to write dialogues. I think from here, he created this thing in his mind that there is some Indian tradition. I have been attacked four times on the street. Still, this casual intellectual racism I faced behind closed doors is far more dangerous because on streets, people might attack you just because you are just different from them. Still, these turuls first segregate you based on culture, region, country, religion, etc. and then they plan the attack. After this incident, I was sent for therapy like many other students who they think are not doing well in new places, but I think there should be "compulsory sensitivity classes" for them. They claim to be teaching in 3-4 universities. they claim to have taught students from all around the world, but all this is nonsense in front of their behavior. He was excited when a Nepalese student was in class because he was teaching one for the first time. We are not lab rats, and we should definitely not be treated like one by these turuls.

CHAPTER FIVE

THE BUTCHER OF AMRITSAR/AZ AMRITSZÁRI HENTES

"*Note: I added this story because it shows the long-term effects of oppression.*"

2.39 : 1

General Reginald Dyer On April 13, 1919, 50 troops under his leadership, all armed with.303 Lee-Enfield rifles opened fire on a nonviolent assembly of thousands of unarmed civilians, men, women, the elderly, and children at the Jallianwalla Bagh. Interestingly, there was no immediate reprimand for Dyer's conduct at Amritsar; on the contrary, on 8 May 1919, he was sent on active service in command of a brigade on the Afghanistan frontier. After the clamor for action against him post-Hunter Commission report grew, he was sent back to Britain. Nigel Collett, in the biography "The Butcher of Amritsar," writes, "NCOs from all units in Jullundur (Jalandhar) — without an order— on April 6, came together to give a warm send off to the officer they respected". Nobel prize laureate Rudyard Kipling hailed him as "the man who saved India."

He died of cerebral hemorrhage and arteriosclerosis on 23 July 1927. Sometimes, I think he got the divine justice he deserved, but then I think it was an easy death compared to the people he murdered in the Jallianwala Bagh Massacre

Udham Singh, an eyewitness to the Jallianwala Bagh massacre, was so horrified by the atrocities of British rule that he dedicated his life to the liberation of India. On 13 March 1940, Shaheed Sardar Udham Singh killed Michael O'Dwyer in London. Dwyer was the Lieutenant Governor of Punjab at that time and he was the one who gave orders to Dyer.

During his trial for assassinating O'Dwyer, he gave his name as Ram Mohammad Singh Azad, which was also tattooed on his arm, signifying that all religions are united against British rule. He also took oath on Waris Shah's Heer-Ranjha, the famous love story of Punjab, a copy of which he had already procured from a *Gurdwara.

"Gurdwara: A Sikh place of worship. From Punjabi Gurduārā"

During the trial, one judge stated, "You are only entitled to say why the sentence of death should not be passed upon you. You are not entitled to make a political speech."

To this, Singh shouted, "I do not care about the sentence of death. It means nothing at all. I do not care about dying or anything. We are suffering from the British Empire... I am standing before an English jury in an English court. You people go to India, and when you come back, you are given prizes and put into the House of Commons, but when we come to England, we are put to death." Singh went on that when the British came to India, they call themselves "intellectuals" and "rulers" and "they order machine guns to fire on Indian students without hesitation." "I have nothing against the public at all. I have more English friends in England than I have in India. I have nothing against the public. I have great sympathy with the workers of England, but I am against the dirty British government," he said (as quoted in the book "Shaheed Udham Singh Di Jeevan-Gatha" by Navtej Singh)

CHAPTER SIX

THE COMPLAINT

Hungarian title: Turul és más futóbolondok az Egyetemről

Translation: Turul and other running fools from the University

Note: Hungarian title is a reference to the 2015 film "Anyám és más futóbolondok a családból (International title: Mom and Other Loonies in the Family)"

1.37:1

So in November 2019, I decided to file an official complaint against him. I also sent them all the emails and Facebook chats along with the complaint.

I received an email a few days later;

""Based on the announcement made by Singh Sidaq Pratap (Neptun Code: RXIO16) student (hereinafter: Student) on November 21, 2019, subject to Section IX./3. of the Ethical Code of the Budapest Metropolitan University, I hereby
order an ethical procedure and its suspension at the same time.

There were many problems in the complaint file. There were many things that I never said or wrote like I never mentioned anything about the Diploma film. So I sent them an email so they can rectify these things.

My email (3.12.2019):

and teaching staff which effected my relationship with other teachers and staff members. I don't have any issues with any other teacher and this misconception is severely damaging my education.

3) I used "racism" word in the emails I shared with you but this is not the keyword which I will use to address this issue. My main concerns are the discriminating behaviour of the teacher and the insensitive email sent to me on 1ˢᵗ October.

4) Another thing I was told my other teachers that He accused me of trying to spoil his reputation but I have only discussed this matter with concerned authorities. I never made this issue public either in private life or on social media

5) I never mentioned anything about my Diploma Film. ""

Their reply:

""Dear Sidaq,

As per your last mail, please have my answer below.

I received the documentation of your issue with your declaration to initiate the Ethical pocedure from Gabor Szabó Lifestile Councelor. Regarding your request I started the procedure. There will be a personal hearing on this procedure and you – as a complainant (and obviosly your teacher) – will have opportunity to explain your point of view detailed.

Since you stated to have exams and to travel home, I plan this personal hearing after your return to Budapest. Before this personal hearing your correction of the complaint below will be sent to the Etics Committee.

As a Secretary General of the University, I wish you a successful exam period and a great winter holiday.""

When I returned, I sent them an email

""Dear Mam
I have returned to Budapest and I available for the hearings and other procedure.""

They replied that

"" they will notify soon"*"

but there was no reply for two months because of the Lockdown and Covid-19.

These six months were very difficult, like when I was telling the direction teacher about myself and I told them that I have a scar on the cornea of one eye and because of this I stayed in a room for two years and she said "teacher". That's why you find it difficult to cooperate with others." They also called me a "dictator" because I requested that Turul not be part of the panel that would judge my this semester's project as it would not be appropriate after the complaint I filed plus my seniors told me that he would try to take his revenge there. After several requests, I was told I didn't have to make any new projects and would be given grade 3 based on my previous projects.

In Panjabi, there is the phrase "Pallā chaḍā'uṇā," which means"to get rid of [Something/Someone]", They all did that with me and never took anything I said seriously.

This reminded me of a story. A Roma lady in Budapest wanted to use the washroom of a famous fast food chain that was "free for everyone," but a security guard was not letting her use it because of her ethnicity. When there was too much noise, some people took out their mobile phones and started shooting. To do damage control, the manager let that lady use the washroom and gave her a free burger.

Their "3" grade out of five was like that free burger for me.

In March 2020, the university's website published an interview with Turul titled "Akikre büszkék vagyunk/Ő is nálunk tanít [Who we are proud of/He also teaches with us]." The article celebrated the presence of a faculty member who had recently been accused of misconduct by a student. After reading this interview, I lost faith in management.

After all this drama, I withdrew my complaint and left the university.

I wrote an Email to the General Secretary:

""THE PRESENT CIRCUMSTANCES HAS MADE ME RECONSIDER the issue I forwarded last semester. I want to withdraw my complaint as the COVID-19 situation has shown me that we all are going through a very difficult phase in life and we should forget and forgive easily. I have been humbled by this situation and it requires us to stand together and fight.
Sidaq Pratap Singh
RXIO16""

They replied

"Dear Sidaq,

Thank you for your kind words, your thoughts are shared by the University.

The ethical procedure in your case has been initiated upon your application. The Hungarian legislation allows the applicants to withdraw their application, so the University shall take the necessary steps to terminate the ethical procedure concerning you complaint.*

**According to Section 47 Paragraph (1)/e) of the Act CL of 2016 on the Code of General Administrative Procedure the authority shall terminate the procedure if the procedure was commenced upon application and each applicant party has withdrawn his application (...).*

Wishing you good health, and successful studies."

CHAPTER SEVEN

DANCE INDIA DANCE

Hungarian title: A Tánc

"*Translation: The Dance*

Note: The Hungarian title is a reference to the first Hungarian film 'A Tánc' (The Dance), directed by Béla Zsitkovszky.

- *Zsitkovszky, Béla (director) (30 April 1901). A Tánc [The Dance] (Motion picture). Kingdom of Hungary*

1.33:1

In the 2016 Hindi language comedy film ''Housefull 3'' a character develops "Dissociative identity disorder (When the psychiatrist says you have DID, the character asks, "What Dance India Dance", an Indian dance reality show). The character develops another personality that replaces him whenever someone says the word "Indian." Because the character was harmed and bullied all his life because of his race and colour, this second personality's job was to create situations where the first personality would be physically harmed.

I never thought this ridiculous scene from this film would become my reality one day. I don't have "DID". It's rare, but a parasite entered my mind. Someone who had no idea about what "culture" was trying to teach me the meaning of "culture." I stopped that parasite from entering my mind the way he wanted to, but he entered my mind in many other ways. These parasites have a sadistic way of segregating people. They claim to be liberal and independent but are poisonous fruit from the same tree they claim to be fighting. With. They call themselves "Cosmopolitan," but in reality, they are "Jack of all cultures, master of none. They create their narrative about culture and want you to adjust according to that. They are like "Modern Colonists." These people do not take away your land but your mind and soul.

I was told that "If I want to work in Indian style, I should find a school in India. He was trying the old colonial trick where we Indians are told that our style is different, it will not work here, and we should change it, and because of our colonial past, we start believing them. Please Don't let these Parasites tell you who you are and where you belong. I ignored this parasite 3-4 times in class, but when he sent that email on 1st October 2019, he crossed all the limits, and there was a need to put a full stop to that nonsense. They know they can say or do anything because a system protects them from everything. Like when I filed a complaint against him, a teacher asked me four times from, "Which part of India I am?" So that they can adjust their parameters for future students coming from my region (This was the direction teacher); another teacher was constantly talking about India to me when I was talking about the teacher because they thought the problem was with me and I was not able to adjust to the new country. (the psychologist who was head of the grievance department and the person who added false claims in the report so that they could defend the Turul) These parasites know these loopholes and hide behind this system. A system that "Systematically destroys a Brain" as they don't have any replacement for these parasites

The direction teacher (let's call her Black Violet, which is what Google translates her name to when we search it on the net) called me a lot of things like "Dictator" when I requested that Turul should not be present during my presentation as it will be a major conflict of interest issue after I filed the complaint. It was like Turul was using her as a weapon, as he could not directly attack me now. I heard that she started using me as a bad example reference when I left. I was disappointed to hear it but recently I read a review about a film they made in 2001, in which it was written "The director has claimed that the film is a call to kiss goodbye to ideologies of all kind, and especially to stop killing or dying for them. Bewilderingly, she nevertheless seemed pleased that a majority of the audience members at a post-screening talk at the Chicago film festival had understood it to take the Croats' struggle against the Serbs between 1992 and 1993 as a just war. Even more puzzling, she was happy to be told by a Croat ex-combatant in the audience that she had depicted the war "exactly as it was." This may be so, but one would expect the director to acknowledge that in a situation in which perspectives are as polarized as this war "telling it as it was" must be subjective and have nothing to do with objectivity. Failing to do so, the film becomes disingenuous as well as naïve. (written by Felicitas Becker for the Kinoeye magazine).

CHAPTER EIGHT

MY LAST ASSIGNMENT

Hungarian title: kívülálló (Outsider)

1.66:1

My last assignment was an essay on retired Hungarian filmmaker Béla Tarr titled "Béla Tarr and the outsiders"

"

Bela Tarr (1955-) made 9 films starting from Family Nest (Családi tüzfészek 1979) and announced his retirement with The Turin Horse (A torinói ló 2011). He starts his career with "social drama" films inspired from Cinéma vérité but later developed his own style or language which would be known as "Tarr Style" His films have been always about an outsider. An outsider who sees things happening around him and knows the consequences of those things but is helpless to prevent that catastrophe. If you talk about Damnation (Kárhozat, 1987) , the first scene is from the point of view of Karrer who is watching the cable cars from his window and Tarr tries to show everything from that perspective with a long shot establishing the importance of a non living thing which could be root cause of various factors in a society. The interior space plays an important role in Tarr's world especially in the case of Damnation, Karrer's life is projected thourh interior spaces both physically and spiritually. His room , the bar and the house of the singer are the three sides of triangle his life revolves around. And we get the feeling that the characters including Karrer are constantly in an interior fight with themselves to know the reason of their existence . There are also external elements like "Rain" but he never tried to use it as a symbol or tried to romanticize it.

It was interesting to watch Tarr's films as an "outsider" as I watched Damnation before his first feature film Family nest (Családi tüzfészek, 1979) and was able to observe a growth or a style which he further expanded in Damnation which the locals might have expericed in 8 years and 3 films between them (The Outsider, The Prefab People and the Almanac of Fall) . In Family nest you will see an external problem , the couple and their issue with the apartment however this recurring them only acts like a salt for taste in this film and the rest of the story of the film characters' response and behavior towards each other, There is a clear sense of documentary style filmmaking or cinema Cinéma vérité which was established in 1960s Europe and came to Hungary in early 1970s. In his book "The Cinema of Bv©la Tarr: The Circle Closes, András B. Kovács describes Family nest as a Film without any physical acts and the film working only on verbal ones.

With Damnation Tarr started a cinematic style that would later be named as "Tarr style". It was also the beginning of his collaboration with writer, and novelist László Krasznahorkai, who wrote the film, and Medvigy. With this film, Tarr started using his famous long shots to create an atmosphere of restlessness and an enchanting progression which ends with a silent viewer slowly emerging from the light and shadow as his surroundings appear steadily which if he compares to his feature Family nest, the films look like with fewer expressions than Damnation and his further Black and White work. We can also analyze the relationship between two environments, the external and the internal where the external environments like the rain, wind, etc. somehow enter the internal elements like doors and floors depicting that how en group psychology can make a layer on an individual's psychology. Somber and surrender words are used to define this film. In the film the setting becomes awful as the film moves forward, and the character inclines towards madness and survival, while it is the affection that drives Karrer crazy, and he wants to do is to push his mind out of the lonely loneliness and his self-practice produces an exhausting environment for others and yet the viewer still sees him moving forward with a determination. Tarr's later films also talk about the concept of humanity with the help of animals like in Damnation Karrer is left barking at a dog.

Despite Tarr's film being set in somewhat deserted world it still gives viewers satirical laugh in a horrible world. You could see an influence of the weather as all his films since 1987 were shot from November to March and were produced by foreigners, adding another layer to his seeing the world from an outsider's perspective. You could observe a very little use of traditional narrative . His this liberal approach was able to create a cosmic world . I was developing my own language, my film language," Tarr acknowledges. "I went deeper and deeper...with The Turin Horse, I arrived at the point where the work is complete, the language is done. I don't want to use my film language for repeating something. I can't. I don't want to be boring.

References

- *Kovács, András Bálint (26 March 2013). The Cinema of Béla Tarr: The Circle Closes .Columbia University Press. ISBN 9780231850377.*
- *Rancière, Jacques (2013). "Béla Tarr, le temps d'après" [Béla Tarr, the Time After].Univocal - University of Minnesota Press (in French). English Translator: Erik Beranek. ISBN 9782918040378.*

"

CHAPTER NINE

TO BE OR NOT TO BE

Hungarian title: A magyar viselkedéskultúra és mentalitás sok elhallgatása és rejtett fel nem tett kérdése

Translation: Many silences and hidden unasked questions of the Hungarian behavioral culture and mentality

Note: The Hungarian title is a reference to a line from the Article "Egy elveszett nyelv" [A lost language]" by Szilárd Borbély

- *"Borbély, Szilárd (5 July 2013). "Egy elveszett nyelv" [A lost language]. Élet és Irodalom (in Hungarian). Vol. 57, no. 27. Budapest. "Azt követően, hogy anyámat az ezredforduló szentestéjén máig ismeretlen rablógyilkosok megölték, és nem vehettem tőle búcsút, sok kérdés merült fel bennem, amelyeket addig nem tettem fel, mert azt hittem, hogy lesz majd alkalmas pillanat. Ugyanis nehéz kérdéseket kellett volna feltennem."[After my mother was killed on the eve of the millennium by unknown robbers and I couldn't say goodbye to her, I had many questions*

*that I didn't ask because I thought the moment would be right.
Because I should have asked difficult questions.]"*

1:1

*"To be, or not to be, that is the question:
Whether 'tis Nobler in the mind to suffer
The Slings and Arrows of outrageous Fortune,
Or to take Arms against a Sea of troubles,
And by opposing end them: to die, to sleep...*

शक प ेहैयकीन तो, यकीन प ेहैशक मुझ े
कसिका झूठ झूठ है, कसिके सच म ेसच नही ं
है की है नही,ं बस यही एक सवाल है
दलि की गर सुन ूतो है, दमिाग की तो है नही ं
जान ल ूक जिान द ू म ैरह ूक ेम ैनही ं

*Shak pe hai yaqeen to, yaqeen pe hai shak mujhe
Kiska jhooth jhooth hai, kiske sach mẽ sach nahī̃
Hai kī hai nahī̃, bas yahī ek savaal hai
Dil kī gar sunū̃ to hai, dimāg kī to hai nahī̃
Jān lū̃ ki jān dū̃, maĩ rahū̃ ki maĩ nahī̃*

*I have faith in my doubt and doubt in faith
Whose lie is a lie, whose truth is not true
Is it or is it not, that's the only question
If I listen to my heart, it's there
if I listen to my mind, though, it's not
Should I take a life, or give mine
should I remain or should I not?*
—

*Original phrase from "Hamlet" and Hindustani language dialogue from the 2014 film "Haider", an adaptation of Hamlet.
References:*

- *Barnet, Sylvan, ed. (1998). Hamlet. Signet Classics. ISBN 9780451526922.*
- *Bhardwaj, Vishal; Peer, Basharat (20 October 2014). Haider: The Original Screenplay (with English Translation). HarperCollins*

India. ISBN 9789351369875

A voice in my mind constantly said, "There was a dream and an ambition that ended." Several dreams were not letting me sleep. In one dream A Turul enters my room and starts attacking me, I try to run to the window to get the turul out and close the window. Then, there was another dream in which I was giving a presentation to Turul and company, and they were making fun of me. Suddenly, there is a pistol in my hand, and I shoot myself.

Thinking of all this, I thought of committing suicide. I thought for days about whether I should die by jumping into a river or jumping off a mountain. I also googled which one of these deaths is less painful. Somedays I used to sit on a bench by the road to select a vehicle to commit suicide. One day I even tried to come under a tram but the driver was able to hit the brake on time and this attempt failed. One of my flatmates had a harakiri samurai sword (harakiri is an act of disemboweling oneself, originally reserved for samurai to die with honor rather than fall into their enemies' hands) and a taser gun. I thought many times that I would use them to kill myself but never got the opportunity. Then I finally went to the hills one day, thinking that I had to commit suicide today in any condition. I was climbing upwards when my foot suddenly slipped, and I fell badly. My whole life came before my eyes. Everything that I had done till now, good or bad, big or small, was spinning in my mind. Everyone, my family and friends were shouting in my mind that I was doing something wrong. I decided to return home.

During an anxiety attack, I used to run toward Liberty Bridge, Picture by Mariam Nizharadze (Instagram account: shoshinfilm)

"Szilárd Borbély (1963 –2014) was a Hungarian academic, writer, and poet. Borbély suffered from "post-traumatic depression" as a result of his mother's death during a burglary in 2000. On the 19th of February, 2014, he committed suicide.

*Borbély's exploration of memory is one of his most remarkable accomplishments. He probed the complex link between memory, identity, and the passage of time, challenging readers to question the accuracy of their memories and the role of common history on moulding individual consciousness. He questioned the common view of memory as a static thing in his writing and poetry, instead depicting it as a changeable construct that changes with time. In the above-mentioned article which was published 7 months before his death, Borbély writes, "**My father survived that dreadful evening, but after six and a half years of loneliness and seclusion, left without saying goodbye owing to unfortunate family circumstances. My father's death was just as senseless and different, but also violent, just like my mother's. But by the time*** *these events occurred, I had long gone forgotten our common language and our conversations were more like memories of former conversations. In any case, our conversations were dominated by the spirit of unquestionable parental respect and filial submission that accepted the law of silence."* (*Translated from Hungarian)* "

""Life in my opinion is a slow suicide. We are all dying a lingering death. This will happen to every intellectual. Whoever is enlightened, this tragedy will remain with him. They are dying every moment"
- Shiv Kumar Batalvi
(Panjabi poet, 1936-1973)

- *Batalvi, Shiv Kumar (1970). "Shiv Kumar Batalvi Exclusive interview with BBC". Nai Zindagi Naya Jeevan (Interview). Interviewed by Mahendra Kaul. London: BBC One.*

Coming back to Turul, there was a senior Indian student who used to write a lot of suicide-related stories and one day, Turul was making fun of him in one of his classes. Soon, the debate turned to suicide rates, and Turul stated that the suicide rate in Hungary is higher than in India, but the Indian student argued that it is higher in India. When the data was checked on the Internet, India was number one on every list. Turul made fun of the Indian students for five minutes, mocking them by calling them mentally weak before changing the subject.

This is the same person who narrates the story of his friend's suicide in every interview, explaining how the accident affected him personally. He even penned a poem on it in an issue of Jelenkor (a literary and art magazine edited in Pécs). However, he mocks others' vulnerability behind closed doors. **Shameless creature**

CHAPTER TEN

LŪHRĪ (LÚRĪ) (PANJABI TITLE)

English Title: Must be the season of the Gerevich

"Note: The English title is a reference to a lyric from the 1966 song "Season of the Witch ." by Scottish singer-songwriter Donovan

- *Leitch, Donovan (2007). The Autobiography of Donovan: The Hurdy Gurdy Man. St. Martin's Press. pp. 133–135. ISBN 978-0312364342.*

Hungarian Title: Titkos kommandós vagyok egy fantáziában

Translation: I'm a secret commando in a fantasy

Note: Hungarian title is a reference to a line from poem "Álmatlanság (Insomnia)" by Turul

- *"Álmatlanság" [Insomnia]. Élet és Irodalom. Vol. 48, no. 15. Budapest (published 9 April 2004). 12 April 2004.*

1:1

"Lūhrī

Language: Panjabi

Meaning: anxiety, apprehension, restlessness; unfulfilled desire, longing, craving."

There is a war I fight every day. An internal struggle that people call anxiety. It's like an inner voice that suppresses me when I am in the crowd by becoming a silent killer and tormenting me with a loud scream whenever I am alone. I try to surround myself with people I love and I keep attempting to erase negativity from my life but even those whom I call "My people" do not understand it, or maybe I am not able to explain it to them. Either they are in complete Denial mode that Nothing happened to me, it's just a fictional thing I created, or they connect every unrelated action to this problem. If I can't explain this problem, then there is no chance I can explain it to the world. I can't explain to them that there is no off button and it never takes any holiday. I prepare myself for the worst scenario every day; it's like something is dying in me every day. It's not easy to "move on," as people tell me each time I share something. It's not I am not trying but whenever someone says "Move on" I feel like I am stuck somewhere, and it suffocates me. Sometimes I am "Ok" but a few moments later I am something I can't explain. Sometimes, People feel that I am attacking them, or sometimes, I feel like I am harming them because it automatically gets triggered, and most of the time, I have no idea what was the trigger point. I need my loved ones by my side in this, but I don't want to be a liability to them. I don't want them to be always in search of a cure for me. I just want them to be the same as me as they were before this war started.

"

Vass nā chalē taqdīr tē hār kē bahi ga'r̃ā
Ājā dil di'ā jānr̃ã shāmã pai ga'r̃ā
"I cannot change anything, and accept my defeat at the hands of fate.
Come already, my darling love, the day has turned to dusk."

– Abdullah Chilli (Pakistani poet and lyricist 1948–) "

CHAPTER ELEVEN

FIUMEI ROAD GRAVEYARD/FIUMEI ÚTI TEMETŐ

1.85 : 1

One day, I reached Fiume Road Cemetery (Hungarian: Kerepesi úti temető) to find life in the house of the dead.

I love these stones in the cemetery. How a sign of one's memory always gives the feeling that someone is there even if they are not. Many people design their graves, and some have their graves prepared by their families. I can never be a part of this realization because I will be burned, but I can think for myself the river in which my ashes will go. From today on, my quest has been to find that river.

"Chār dinã dā mēlā dunī'ã phir māṭṭī dī ḍhērī
The glittering spectacle of this world lasts but a few days And then everything turns to dust"

Grave of Lajos Bardos

Lajos Bárdos (1899-1986) Hungarian composer, conductor, music theorist, and professor.

His work included folk song arrangements, Choral Masses, motets, secular pieces based on poems, theatrical accompaniments, and around

800 instrumental music pieces. He also wrote school books, essays, and theoretical books on music.

Grave of Árpád Tóth

Árpád Tóth (1886–1928) was a Hungarian poet and translator.

"Egy égi üzenet, mely végre most
Hozzám talált, s szememben célhoz ért,
S boldogan hal meg, amíg rácsukom
Fáradt pillám koporsófödelét. (From Lélektől lélekig "From Soul to Soul" written in 1923)

Its heavenly message has arrived, at last,
safe in my sight from wandering through the skies,
and dies content when I upon it cast
the coffin-cover of my weary eyes. (Translation by Watson
Kirkconnell)"
53

"Watson Kirkconnell (1895 – 1977) was a Canadian scholar,
university administrator (Acadia University) and translator."

Thank you so much to Júlia, who took the day off work to go with me to the cemetery to see the tombs of several well-known people. She said she would show me a Jewish cemetery the following time, but sadly, because of the shifting lockdown hours, that day never materialized.

Address book: Fiumei Road Graveyard, Budapest, Fiumei út 16-18,
1086 Hungary

Known and Unknown love story

Hungarian title: Nézzen ki olykor a temetőbe, az elég

"Translation: Look into the cemetery sometimes, that's enough

Note: Hungarian title is a reference to a line from the 1987 novel Az ajtó (The Door) by Magda Szabó.

- *"Szabó, Magda (1987). Az ajtó [The Door]. ISBN 9789631407099"*

- *"Szabó, Magda (15 February 1995). The Door. Translated by Stefan Draughon. East European Monographs/Harvill Secker. ISBN 0-88033-304-9."*

1.85 : 1

Known

Magda Szabó (1917–2007), Hungarian writer, poet, translator, and Tibor Szobotka (1913–1982), Hungarian writer, translator, literary historian, teacher

Magda Szabó is one of the most translated Hungarian authors. Her novel "Abigél (1970)" was made into a popular television show in 1978, and her novel "Az ajtó (The Door, 1987) won many literary prizes.

Tibor Szobotka is a József Attila Prize-winning writer best known for his translation work.

In 1945, Szabó began working at the Ministry of Education. She was dismissed from the ministry during the Stalinist regime of Hungary. She was not allowed to publish his work. From 1949 to 1956. Her novel "The Door" is about a writer who is also the book's narrator, who lives in a Hungarian village with her husband, who is also a writer. Their work was banned for years before the book's start, the ban is lifted. Now she can write again.

Szabó and Tibor got married in 1947. After Tibor died in 1982, Magda wrote his biography Megmaradt Szobotkának (Remaining for Szobotka, 1983), using the available diaries and draft content. The book's text is like a dramatic dialogue in which a grieving wife talks to her deceased partner.

wife is talking to her deceased partner.

Grave of Szabó and Tibor

UNKNOWN

Somewhere in Fiumei Road Graveyard

The husband used to make a sign of the cross with them every Sunday at his wife's grave, and after his death, one or the other of his family members carried on this tradition.

LETTER TO SELF

I love these stones in the cemetery. How a sign of one's memory always gives the feeling that someone is there even if they are not. Many people design their graves, and some have their graves prepared by their families. I can never be a part of this realization because I will be cremated, and after cremation, the mourner will collect the ashes and consecrate it to a water body, such as a river or sea. But I can think for myself the river or sea in which my ashes will go after cremation. From today on, my quest has been to find that river.

Current Location: Árkod

MARCH 2024

Although physically, I have left Budapest and returned to Jalandhar, mentally, I am in the town called Árkod.

Magda Szabó's novel "Abigél (anglicised: Abigail)" mentions Árkod, a fictional town (not to be confused with the Serbian settlement "Jarkovac," which is called Árkod in Hungarian) in the novel.

In the novel, Georgina "Gina" Vitay, a young girl, is sent to a boarding school in the fictional town of Árkod. The town is described as a town with its distinct atmosphere and residents. In the story, Árkod serves as the backdrop for Gina's coming-of-age adventure, filled with friendships, hardships, and self-discovery. The town's representation adds greatly to the novel's appeal, as it becomes an important element of Gina's personal and emotional landscape.

The one distinction is that Abigail, the "mysterious benefactor" who grants everyone's wishes upon receiving a letter, is absent here.

CHAPTER TWELVE

URBEX/ VÁROSFELFEDEZÉS

1.37:1

According to an article I read recently, more than 50% of Hungary's eateries may soon close their doors. Reading this story brought back memories of riding the tram 4-6. In late 2020, when the government relaxed some traveling rules after the lockdown, many of my pals embarked on an Urbex adventure to explore artificial structures, typically abandoned ruins. However, I was witnessing Budapest becoming a soon-to-be abandoned area. There were hardly any tourists, and the rules changed almost daily. Orders for home delivery were many eateries' only remaining source.

I used to travel daily on tram 4-6 and see restaurant owners waiting for customers or orders with hope in their eyes. After that, I used to go home and order from one of the restaurants. With just one order, they didn't get much financial help, but it was enough to generate hope that good times would come after this time.

I used to receive numcrous thank-you notes along with the order, and many people also sent me special delicacies that could only be stored fresh and were given to me as gifts.

At the time, I was thinking about the escapism of people traveling to visit faraway abandoned buildings while neglecting the destiny of many businesses in their city, which are at risk of becoming abandoned buildings.

Dogs of separation

A homeless man and a dog used to sleep outside a general store on the road I used to pass while going to college. One night during the winter, he was shivering badly, and one of my friends gave him his jacket. After that night, whenever he saw us, he used to show us that he was wearing that jacket and say thank you very loudly.

One day, a lady with a dog passed by that general store, and that homeless man's dog started barking at them. I don't speak Hungarian, but I could understand what that man said to his dog. He asked, where would they go if they were kicked out of that place because of that dog's action? I can bet that he was saying that.

In March 2020, during the lockdown, that man and his dog disappeared like all the homeless people in the city. After six months, I saw them sleeping near Nehru Part, a park near the bank of the Danube. The man recognized me, but the dog couldn't and started barking at me. I was disappointed that he could not recognize me, but at the same time, I was happy to see them alive.

> *"Nehru Part is a park in Budapest named after Jawaharlal Nehru, India's first prime minister. Nehru sympathised with the Hungarian people's struggle during the 1956 Hungarian Revolution, hence the park is named after him in respect. The park near Petőfi Bridge on the bank of the river Danube provides a calm escape with lush greenery and scenic views."*

Hijarã dē kālē sagg mērē utē bhauñkadē dē nẽ lagadā ē mainũ en si'āṇa dē nahĩ mā'ĩ

The black dogs of separation's misery bark at me. It seems like they fail to recognize me and instead think of me as a stranger.

–Shahnawaz Zaidi

Second Innings

Hungarian title: Meg élünk [We are Still Alive]

2.55:1

Meg élünk [We are Still Alive]

Negative thought:

One fine Sunday afternoon you visit a camp currently inhabited by homeless people and you had some quality time with them

The next day you are getting ready to go to the office which is built at the place which was once the home of people, the same ones who are now homeless people you met yesterday.

Positive thought:

I love this city. Many people asked me to return to my country. They were either highly educated people who tried to declare me unfit for this city or they were street drunkards who had a problem with my complexion.

But I always kept thinking that Budapest is a lover from another faith whose political mother and drunken father will never let our love story end on a happy note. It's a different story that I have to leave this country after finishing my studies but I also swear today that after my death my ashes will be scattered here in the Danube River and No stupid parents can stop me from loving this city, me beloved than.

CHAPTER FOURTEEN

Neo-Nazi Moles/ Neonáci Vakondok

"Note: I am adding this story because in the previous protest held on 6.6.2020 I also saw Turul. Thankfully I didn't see him there that day. The only difference between him and Derek Chauvin is that Chauvin attacked physically while he attacked verbally. Both left no stone unturned in misusing their power."

1.37 : 1

So there was a #blm march on 20.6,2020 in Budapest. A day before that, a Library (Közkincs Könyvtár)in Budapest held an event where people were invited to make signs for the BLM event the next day. 6-7 men joined the workshop, all dressed in black, and they refused to take their masks off when requested, but they began making posters, so we gave them the benefit of the doubt. We later came to know that all were from some far-right group after we saw them with a confederate flag at the march. Later, we checked the signs they made, and we discovered that they had hidden white supremacy propaganda in all of their posters. We also discovered that they had stolen box cutters from the library.

In August 2020, the same group tore down two rainbow flags from various buildings during an anti-LGBT march organized by them.

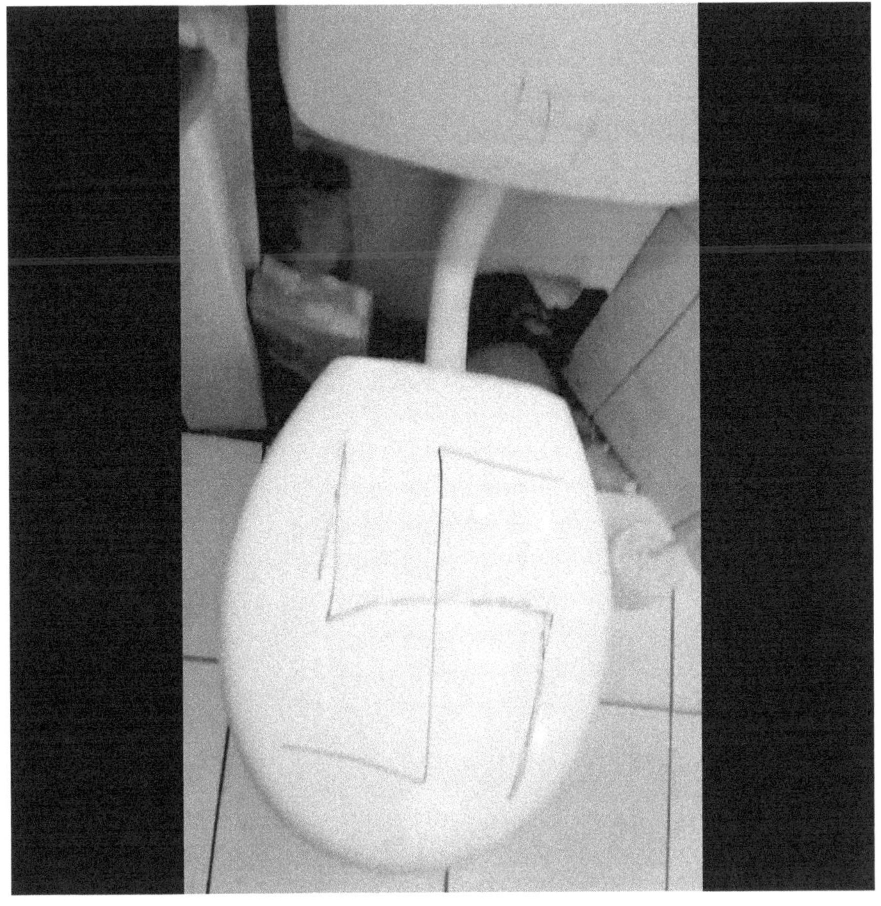

Picture of the Swastika they drew on the Library's toilet seat

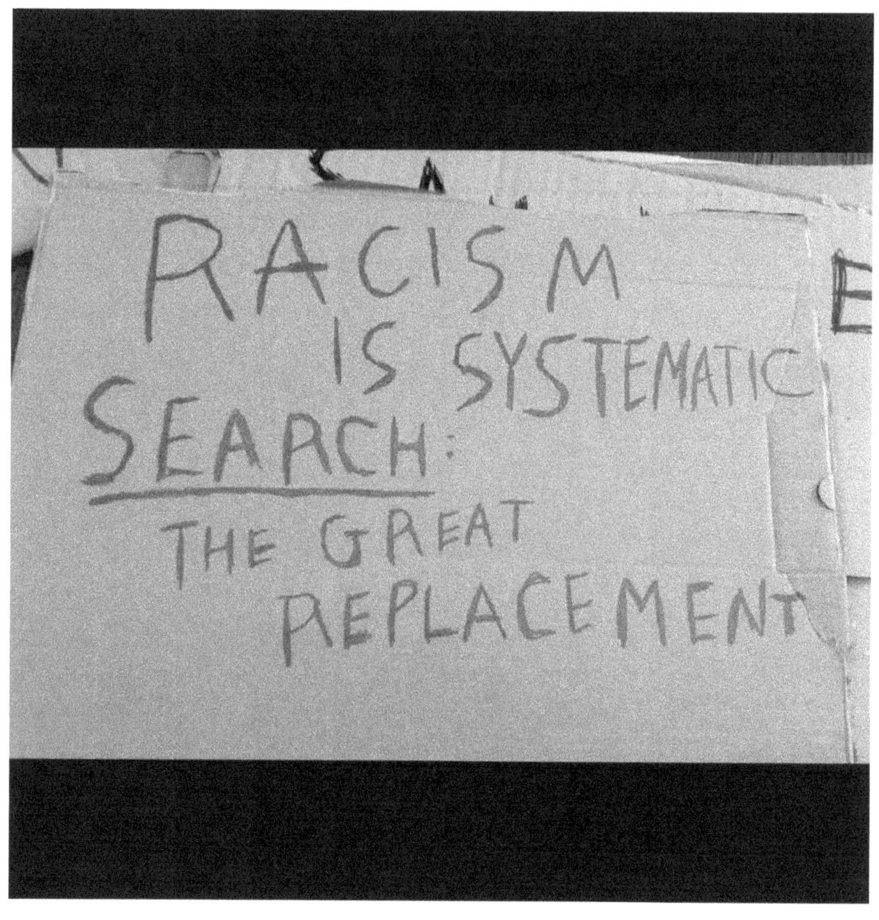

In this picture, they mentioned "The Great Replacement", a white nationalist conspiracy theory that states that white European populations at large are being demographically and culturally replaced with non-European peoples—specifically Arab, Berber, South Asian, and Sub-Saharan populations.

In this one, they mentioned "Siege," an anthology of pro-nazi essays written by American Neo-nazi James Mason.

Antonia Burrows and Közkincs Könyvtár

1.66:1

Antonia Burrows is a British Activist and Owner of Közkincs Könyvtár, a Feminist Library in Budapest. She was also a teacher at ELTE School of English and American Studies in the early to mid-1990s and from 2015 to 2019.

According to the Book Global Gender Research: Transnational Perspectives:

"Antonia Burrows was the first feminist role model for a surprisingly large cohort of later feminist scholars."

In 1994, She was one of the founders of NANE, an emergency service to fight violence against women and children in Hungary. In 2000, Burrows moved to California, where she collected books for 15 years. She returned to Budapest in 2015 and opened the Közkincs Könyvtár, a Library and community place.

My Problem with Antonia

I met Antonia in 2019 and worked as a volunteer in her library for about a year. I have some issues with her, which have not been resolved until now. I wrote a letter expressing my displeasure in 2021. I hope she got it.

First, I thought I would write a chapter on her, titled "Squirrels Running the Government and Tania Head a Library," but then I thought I never got to talk to her face to face. I want to fight her face-to-face first. Right now, I am too weak (both mentally and physically) to fight a wordsmith like Antonia, but when I am in better condition, I will try to talk to her.

Furthermore, discussing certain subjects at this time would be inappropriate because it could benefit the wrong people and generate disruption, causing the movement that has been going on in Hungary for years to suffer. Many people might lose faith in the truth if I share those things publicly. So it's better if some secrets stay with me and end with me.

"Strangely, ELTE School of English and American Studies is somehow connected to every one of my adversaries."

5 August 2020, Budapest

Reciting "Ajj Aakhaan Waris Shah Nu (Ajj ākhā̃ Waris Shah nũ), a dinge about horrors of the partition of the Punjab, written by Amrita Pritam. Also, the last time I met Antonia.

CHAPTER FIFTEEN

DEATH OF SARAH HEGAZI

Hungarian title: "Kimerítettek és megöltek, és az egész társadalom ott állt és tapsolt értük, elvtárs"

Translation: They have exhausted and killed me, and the whole society stood there clapping for them, comrade
Note: The Hungarian title is a translation of lines from the diary of Sarah Hegazi, originally written in Arabic. "

Sarah Hegazi (1989-2020) was a socialist, writer, and LGBT activist from Egypt. Egyptian officials detained and tortured her in 2017 after she flew a rainbow flag at a Mashrou' Leila performance in Cairo. Hegazi suffered from PTSD as a result of her imprisonment and mistreatment in Egypt. She was granted asylum in Canada, a comparatively more tolerant and safe society. However, the wounds of her past plagued her, and she continued to struggle with mental health. She sadly died by suicide in Canada on 14 June 2020.

Her suicide note:

To my siblings, I have tried to find salvation and I failed, forgive me. To my friends, the journey was cruel and I am too weak to resist, forgive me. To the world, you were cruel to a great extent, but I forgive," Translated from Arabic
- Sarah Hegazi

VIgil for Sarah Hegazi

On 25 June 2020, a vigil for Sarah Hegazi was held near Budapest's Liberty Square. Egyptian students from Central European University organized it. One of them, Ahmed Samir Santawy, was arbitrarily detained by Egyptian authorities in January 2021 for his research and study of women's rights, including the history of reproductive rights in Egypt. Still, the charges framed against him were "funding a terrorist organization" and "deliberately spreading false news and data." Ahmed was convicted of spreading "fake news" and sentenced to three years in jail on 4 July 2022, but he was released in August 2022 after receiving a presidential pardon.

I never met Sarah, yet learning of her death was like losing a close relative. Her death was the first impetus for me to "come out."

75

KIBITZER

Hungarian title: Macska város

"*Translation: Cat City*

Note: The Hungarian title is a reference to the international title of the 1986 animated Hungarian film "Macskafogó"

- *Béla Ternovszky (Director), József Nepp (Writer), Román Kunz (Producer) (2 October 1986). Macskafogó [Cat Catcher] (Motion Picture) (in Hungarian). Hungary: J2 Communications / Pannonia Film Studios (Production company), Sefel Pictures Intl (Production company), Infafilm (Production Company), Mokép (Distributor). OCLC 47043093. "International title: Cat City "*

2.39:1

Screening of two short films by Syrian filmmaker Haydar Slyteen at MiraDoor

On 6 October 2020. I attended a Screening of two short films by Syrian filmmaker Haydar Slyteen at MiraDoor. After the screening, Slyteen said that if someone asks him about the situation in Syria, he says that the situation there is like the film "Mad Max: Fury Road (2015)."

"The Syrian conflict has triggered a major humanitarian disaster. Millions of people have been domestically displaced or have become refugees in neighbouring countries and beyond. There have been extensive claims of human rights violations, including the use of

chemical weapons and indiscriminate airstrikes."

The "Syrian conflict" is a real-world geopolitical crisis with complex historical and political roots, whereas "Mad Max: Fury Road" is a fictitious post-apocalyptic dystopian film. Both, however, share the themes of authoritarianism, scarcity of resources, revolt, and the desire for freedom and justice in a world of turmoil and bloodshed.

Turul also wrote a poem on the Aleppo bombings in 2016. After reading that poem, I posted on Facebook:

"

Ehdē vargē McDonald's varžan bahut milaṇagē tuhānū yūropī deshã vich. Eh matalabī lōk siraf āpaṇā pōrṭfōli'ō baṇā'uṇā jāṇdē han, Ehnã nū dūjē lōkã dē dukh darad nāḻ kō'ī matalab nahī̃. (Panjabi)

Számos hozzá hasonló McDonald's változatot találhat az európai országokban. Ezek az önző emberek csak azt tudják, hogyan készítsék el saját portfóliójukat, nem törődnek mások fájdalmával és szenvedésével. (Hungarian)

Translation: You will find a lot of McDonald's versions like him in European countries. These mean people only know how to make their own portfolios, they don't care about the pain and suffering of other people. "

Similarly, If a Hungarian asks me to describe my life in Hungary, I say it's like the animated film "Cat City" (Macskafogó, 1986). Directed by Béla Ternovszky, "Macskafogó," aka "Cat City" in the English-speaking world, combines film noir, slapstick comedy, and satire elements. Set in the year 80 AM (Anno Mickey Mouse), the story follows the ambitious and cunning cat mobster as he plots to take over the city's criminal underworld. His efforts, however, are foiled by a mouse detective.

"Macskafogó" offers a comical yet insightful perspective on modern Hungarian culture. While the film's depiction of anthropomorphic animals in a crime-ridden metropolis is fictitious, it deftly touches on themes and situations still relevant in Hungary. The film depicts a city in disarray and corruption, mirroring societal issues like crime. Urban centers in contemporary Hungary have had their issues, including increased crime rates in some places and worries about governmental corruption.

"Macskafogó" uses satire to comment on the portrayal of morally ambiguous characters in media. Political satire has also been an important component of public debate in modern Hungary. Political leaders and institutions are frequently criticised through satirical programmes, cartoons, and political humour, stressing the significance of freedom of speech in the country.

In 2018, **Kovács M. David** of **Index** wrote, "Although not all works of art stand the test of time, Macskafogó has aged well. That is why we return to it so willingly. " (Translated from Hungarian)

Building with Cat City artwork

"Event:

Útilapu Hálózat - SCI Hungary; Open Doors Hungary; Mira Intercultural Community; Haydar Slyteen (6 October 2020). "Short films screening - Haydar Slyteen". www.facebook.com. "

CHAPTER SEVENTEEN

WHAT I WAS THINKING AFTER THESE TWO EVENTS

Hungarian title: 2020.VI. 26.

2.39 : 1

26.6.2020

I went to two events in the past seven days. Such voices have sometimes raised hopes that the world is not so bad. As I walk towards my destination, I see many faces on the road turning towards me. Many people find me gypsy and have problems with my beard. I have been attacked four times on the road, but this thing did not discourage me because I know how to fight these people, but these people are not the real danger. Some other people are spreading the real poison. You will find these people sitting in government offices who have entirely forgotten the thing called humanity in the intoxication of money and power. You will see some of them as teachers in schools and universities wearing fake masks. My real battle is with them now.

SAY NO
TO RACISM
EVERY DAY

SILENCE
=
COMPLIANCE

I SEE U
I HEAR U
I'M BY
YOUR
SIDE

BLM Protest

Vigil for Sarah Hegazi Budapest, 25.6.2020

CHAPTER EIGHTEEN

Hungary 2021

Some glimpses of what was happening in Hungary before my return to Jalandhar in March 2021.

Anti LGBT LAW

A children's book called "Meseország mindenkié (Fairytaleland is for Everyone)" which was written to increase acceptance of homosexuals, was torn and shredded in September 2020 by Dóra Dró, a member of the Hungarian National Assembly, who called it "homosexual propaganda."

In June-July 2021, The Hungarian government introduced "Act LXXIX of 2021" often mentioned as " Hungarian anti-LGBT law". The law prohibits the depiction of LGBTQ+ in places where children could be (basically everywhere)

The EU Commission Launched infringement procedures against Hungary related to equality and the protection of fundamental rights.

"Europe will never allow parts of our society to be stigmatised: be it because of whom they love, because of their age, their ethnicity, their political opinions, or their religious beliefs.

President Ursula von der Leyen, (European Parliament, 7 July 2021)"

Háttér Society (Háttér Társaság in Hungarian) has received multiple reports since the adoption of the law. As per the organization, "Verbal violence is the most common, but sometimes they are approached for pushing and other physical insults. According to the case manager, many people feel empowered by the law to abuse members of sexual minorities."

*"Háttér Society (Háttér Társasg in Hungarian, háttér means background) is an NGO representing LGBTQI people i'n Hungary. It operates a telephone hotline and a legal aid service. Háttér is member of " Hungarian LGBT Alliance", a seven member organization that brings together LGBTQI organizations in Hungary. (other organizations include, *Atlasz Lesbian, Gay, Bisexual and Transgender Sport Association, *Labrisz Lesbian Association, *Patent Association, *Szimpozion LGBT Youth Association, *Rainbow Mission Foundation, *Rainbow Families Foundation)"*

Some of my queer friends were evicted from their apartments without any notice even though there was still time for their rental agreement to expire.

Who all will be affected by this law, according to a factsheet by **Forbidden Colours,** a Belgian NGO:

- *"Children: LGBTIQ+ children are more likely to become victims of bullying and violence in school, at home and in social media."*
- *"Teacher: Teachers are prevented from providing objective and pluralistic relatioships and sex education."*
- *"Media and Artists: Journalists' and artists cannot impart information and ideas without the interference of public authorities."*
- *"LGBTIQ NGOs: LGBTIQ-led NGOs and Pride NGOs operating space is restricted and their donors might feel discouraged to donate."*
- *"Entrepreneurs: Self-employed persons and entrepreneurs are unlawfully limited in their right to provide media, advertising and training services in Hungary"*

Law:

2021. évi LXXIX. törvény: a pedofil bűnelkövetőkkel szembeni szigorúbb fellépésről, valamint a gyermekek védelme érdekében egyes törvények módosításáról [LXXIX of 2021 law: on stricter action against pedophile offenders and on the amendment of certain laws for the protection of children]

Index

Index.hu is a well-known Hungarian news website established in 1999. It is regarded as one of Hungary's most prominent and frequently read internet news sites. The index covers various topics, including politics, economics, culture, sports, and international news.

The editor-in-chief's resignation in 2020 raised questions about the website's independence and journalistic freedom. This episode resulted in the departure of numerous journalists and sparked debates in Hungary concerning press freedom.

Szabolcs Dull stepped down as Index's editor-in-chief on July 22, 2020, following a series of disputes and concerns about its editorial independence.

The resignation occurred after the website's popular and long-serving head editor, Gábor Máthé, was fired in June 2020. The dismissal of Máthé prompted worries among journalists and readers about the possible influence of the Index's editorial independence. The conflict centered on control of the website's financial and editorial activities. Index was majority-owned by the organization for the Future of Index (Index-jövért Alaptvány), a private organization designed to protect the news outlet's independence and financial stability. Tensions emerged when a new chairman was appointed to the foundation, who was seen by many as having political connections to Hungary's ruling party.

Following Szabolcs Dull's departure, nearly 70 journalists and staff members resigned in solidarity, citing their fears about Index's future. This enormous exodus severely impacted the website's functioning and reputation. Index resumed operations with a smaller workforce and worked to reconstitute its editorial team following the mass resignations. However, the episode was a watershed moment in the website's existence, creating a lasting impression on Hungary's media landscape and highlighting the obstacles that independent journalism faces in the nation.

Translation: Index there is no other

Free SZFE

"Free SZFE" is a series of protests and clashes surrounding the University of Theatre and Film Arts (Színház- és Filmművészeti Egyetem, or SZFE) in Hungary. After the Hungarian government announced substantial modifications to the university's governance structure in 2020, worries regarding academic freedom and autonomy arose.

The Hungarian government approved legislation in July 2020 that moved ownership and operation of SZFE from the autonomous public body that previously managed it to a new foundation. Critics argued that the alteration weakened the university's autonomy and allowed for political influence in its operations. Students, alumni, faculty members, and supporters of SZFE held rallies and demonstrations under the slogan "Free SZFE" to condemn the government's actions. They feared that the alterations jeopardized academic freedom, artistic integrity, and the university's independence.

CHAPTER NINETEEN

BÚCSÚZIK

I was five years old when I saw the film Sadma [transl. Trauma] (1983).

In this film the character Somu saves Reshmi (Nehalata) who suffers from retrograde amnesia from a brothel. He takes her to *Ooty and takes full care of her. When Reshmi finally recovers from the amnesia, she forgets everything that happened between her accident and the treatment, including the way Somu took care of her. Somu tried a lot to remind her of that past but Nehlalata thinks he is insane and ignores all his efforts.

The reason I was shocked to see this film was because I was seeing this kind of separation for the first time. I knew death because I had witnessed my grandmother's death when I was three years old, but this kind of separation in which the person is alive but still distant and out of reach was a new thing for a five-year-old. I did not sleep many nights after watching this film.

When I was heading to the airport from my flat. This film was playing in my head, and I thought the city was trying to stop me. It seemed as if Budapest was trying to remind me of all the wonderful times we had together, but I had no choice but to leave with a promise to return someday.

Famous Panjabi writer and Poet, in her Memoir "Raseedi Ticket (The Revenue Stamp)," wrote:

"A hundered and Twenty kilometers to the south oF Budapest, I see the side of Lake Balaton where on November 6, 1926. Tagore wrote had planted a sapling and had written "May this add to each new season of yours even when I have passed away from this earth." A statue of Tagore stands nearby with the full verse inscribed on the pedestal, however it is dated November 8, 1926. I take a leaf off the tree and seem to read instead the date September 8, 1967 engraved

on it.... (Translated from Panjabi)"

Before departing, I inscribed my name with an imaginary pen on a leaf, hoping it would fly through the Budapest breezes like Forrest Gump's floating feather.

"Amrita Pritam (1919-2005) was an Indian author, essayist, and poet who wrote in both Punjabi and Hindi. She is most recognised for her poignantpoetry and prose, which frequently explore themes of love, partition, and women's problems in society. She wrote nearly a hundred volumes, including poetry collections, novels, essays, and biographies. Some of her outstanding works include "Ajj Aakhaan Waris Shah Nu" ("I Call Upon Waris Shah Today"), published in the aftermath of India's Partition in 1947, which is a sad lament over the violence and suffering caused by the event."

CHAPTER TWENTY

LETTER TO UNCLE JERICHO BROWN

Open Letter to American poet Jericho Brown, written in September 2023

1:1

Saadat Hasan Manto (1912-1955) was a Pakistani writer, playwright, and author who is considered among the greatest writers of short stories in South Asia. In 1951, he wrote a letter to Uncle Sam (USA), and now, after 70+ years, I am writing a letter to Sam's son, Jericho Brown.

Jericho Brown (1976-) is a contemporary American poet. Brown has worked as an educator at institutions such as the University of Houston, San Diego, and Emory University. He has won several accolades throughout his career, including the Pulitzer Prize for Poetry in 2020 for his collection "The Tradition." Turul has translated many of Jericho Brown's poems into Hungarian.

"

99 Bank Colony,
Behind Verka Milk Plant
Jalandhar, 144008

15 September 2023

Dear Uncle,

Greetings,

I heard your poems explore topics like race and identity. But do you know that a racist person is translating your poetry in a distant country called Hungary?

There is a slight difference of course, Derek Chauvin did a physical attack and Turul's attacks were verbal. I tried to die many times but failed. Maybe this is my mistake, if I had taken my life then maybe poets like you would have written a lot of poems on that tragedy.

I have no idea if this letter will reach you and if it reaches you, you will take any action or not. Because the attacker is from your community (writer, poet, Professor) and the person who was attacked (me) is from a different part of the world and is of different color. Kevin Dave was heard saying that people of my skin color have "limited value" in your country.*

The reason I am writing this letter to you is because there was some emphasis on resilience and hope in your poetry. I've written a number of letters to "concerned authorities" over the years, but to no result. This time, I decided to write a letter to a person who lives 8,000 kilometres away and is known to confront the harsh realities of Racism in his poetry.

If after reading this letter you feel that you cannot do anything, then at that time forward the above address to András and tell him to send a henchman that can free me from this pain.

Uncle I've also heard that you use biblical allusions to express a deeper social or emotional meaning. If we were never able meet in this life and I pass away before you, I'll wait for you in Sheol and ask if you read my letter and what you did afterward.

Your poor nephew

Sidaq Pratap Singh ”

*On January 23, 2023, Kandula was killed at Dexter Avenue North and Thomas Street when Officer Kevin Dave hit her while responding to an overdose call. Kevin Dave drove 74 mph in a 25-mph zone just before he hit Kandula. Dave appeared to joke and burst into laughing at the death of an Indian student, as captured by his body camera. He can be heard saying, "She is dead," before bursting into laughter. "Yeah, just write a check. Eleven thousand dollars. She was 26 anyway," he further said, "She had limited value" towards the end of the clip.

In February 2024, it was reported that Kevin Dave would not face criminal charges due to a lack of "sufficient" evidence.

Intermission

PART 2

COMING SOON

Mērē gīt vī lōk suṇĩndē nē
nālē kāfar ākh sadĩndē nē
maĩ dard nũ Kā'abā kahi baiṭhā
Rabba nã rakkh baiṭhā pīṛ dā

People listen to my songs and then address me as a "*Kafir". I addressed all my pain "*Kaaba" and named all my sufferings "God."

\- **Shiv Kumar Batalvi**
(Panjabi poet, 1936-1973)

*"*Kafir (Arabic origin): Infidel, Disbeliever*

**Kaaba (Arabic origin :al-Ka'bah): building at the center of Islam's most important mosque, the Masjid al-Haram in Mecca, Saudi Arabia."*

Acknowledgements

Thank you to my parents, Sardar Harmeet Singh and Sophia Chattwal, and my sister Rashmika; thank you to Anna Szirmai, Meriem Fgaier, and Govind Oberoi for always being there for me in Budapest. Pantea Pakniyat and Jainuddin Shaikh were prominent supporters during the Turul Saga. Thank you to Ridhima Sharma (Instagram: ridhimasharma.illustrates) for the beautiful book cover. Thank you, Niki Karagianni, Mariam Nizharadze, and Roland Szabó, for allowing me to use their images.

Image courtesy: Roland Szabó (Instagram:rolandszabo.photo)

Endnotes

Names

- ˈɒnːɒ ˈlindɒ ˈsirmɒi

Anna is a female name of Latin origin, mostly in reference to St Anne, the apocryphal mother of Mary, mother of Jesus, but appears in the Vulgate (Latin translation of the Bible) as a reference to Anna the Prophetess. Name day: July 26

> "Hungarians celebrate birthdays and name days! Name days are special days celebrated on a day designated for particular names. These days are picked mainly based on religious traditions and historical events, celebrated in the workplace and among friends."

- t̪ɪl̪l̪ot̪əma ʃoɱe

Tillottama is the name of an Apsara (female spirit) featured in Mahabharata.

- ˈbɛaːtɒ ˈfɒl

Beáta is a female name of Latin origin. Meaning: happy. Name day: March 8, 22; June 24, 29; September 6; December 16.

- soʊˈfi.ə t͡ʃʰət̪yaːl

Sophia is a female name of Ancient Greek origin. My Mother Got her name from the Russian Novella **"Sofia Petrovna " by Lydia Chukovskaya.**

- ˈkɒt̪ɒlin ˈɒknɒI

Katalin is a female name of Greek origin. Its meaning is pure. The Hungarian version of the Greek name "Αικατερίνη (Aikateriné)". It probably entered Hungarian via the German "Katharina" or the Latin "Catharina" form. Name day: April 30; November 25.

- ˈgaːbor ˈkɛrtvi:

Gábor is a Hungarian male given name, equivalent to English Gabriel. Name Day: March 24.

- ˈdʒɔɹdʒ ˈsɪərtɛʃ

Szirtes is a Hungarian surname. In Hungarian, it primarily refers to someone from "szirt," a cliff or rocky place. It is also the Hungarian name of the village Strihovce in Slovakia.

- uːɖʱəm sɪŋ (anglicised version)
- əm.mrɪʈɑː pɾiːʈəm

Amrita is Sanskrit origin female origin word which means immortal

Aspect Ratios:

- 2.39:1—This wider aspect ratio is commonly associated with epic and grandiose storytelling. It enables broad landscapes and panoramic perspectives, making it ideal for action sequences and visually stunning situations. Films shot in this ratio frequently provide a feeling of scale and grandeur.

- 1.66:1—In comparison, the 1.66:1 aspect ratio is slightly taller and narrower. It is frequently used for more intimate stories, emphasising characters and their relationships. This aspect ratio creates a balanced frame that highlights the characters' emotions and relationships within the composition. Films in this ratio may feel more intimate and engaging because the narrower frame draws attention to the characters and their experiences.

- 1.78:1 – The 1.78:1 aspect ratio is wider and more rectangular than 1.66:1 and corresponds to the size of modern television and digital screens. This ratio frequently conveys a sense of contemporary storytelling and connection to current events. Themes linked with 1.78:1 can include modernism, accessibility, and versatility in storytelling across numerous genres and platforms.

- 1.33:1 – This aspect ratio was widely used in the early days of cinema and is connected with classic films and television broadcasts. It features a square-ish frame that feels balanced and adaptable. Films shot in this ratio frequently prioritise storytelling through people and conversation above visual spectacle. It might evoke nostalgia and intimacy since it recalls the golden age of cinema.

- 1.37:1 – The Academy of Motion Picture Arts and Sciences standardised this aspect ratio, sometimes called the Academy ratio, in 1932. It is slightly wider than 1.33:1, yet remains more square than recent widescreen formats. This ratio frequently has a classic and timeless vibe, similar to those of the golden age of Hollywood. This aspect ratio can convey a sense of balance and stability, making it appropriate for various storytelling techniques.

- 1:1 – This aspect ratio is square, with equal width and height. It is frequently connected with social media platforms such as Instagram, where square photographs are common. Films in this aspect ratio can feel experimental and unorthodox since they violate typical cinematic norms. It can provide a sense of symmetry and balance within the frame, allowing for innovative compositions and visual storytelling approaches. Xavier Dolan chose to shoot his film "Mommy (2014)" in a 1:1 aspect ratio to increase the emotional intensity and intimacy of the film. The square aspect ratio shows claustrophobia and immediacy, highlighting the characters' intimacy and emotional interactions.

- 2.55:1 – The original Cinemascope aspect ratio, established in the 1950s, produced a substantially wider image than the normal Academy ratio of 1.37:1. Later, the aspect ratio was significantly decreased to 2.35:1 to accommodate technical upgrades and address issues like frame distortion. It could show juxtaposed elements, convey visual metaphors, or highlight thematic contrasts.

References

- Anna Szirmai. mentalkozpont.hu. MentálKözpont. 1 September 2017
- After tense Germany trip, Erdogan set for warm reception in Hungary". France24. Budapest. AFP. 8 October 2018.
- "Dr. Aknai Katalin PhD | Pécsi Tudományegyetem". art.pte.hu. University of Pécs.
- Farley, Paul (4 February 2005). "A world of memory: Paul Farley salutes George Szirtes, a worthy winner of the 2004 TS Eliot prize with Reel". The Guardian.
- "Maintenant #86 " (Interview). Interviewed by SJ Flower. Budapest: Poetry International Online. 9 September 2013
- Collett, Nigel (2006). The Butcher of Amritsar. Continuum. ISBN 978-1852855758.
- Singh, Navtej (2016). Shaheed Udham Singh Di Jeevan-Gatha [Life story of Shaheed Udham Singh] (in Punjabi). Unistar Books. ISBN 978-9352043866.
- Shoojit Sircar (Director), Shubhendu Bhattacharya (Writer), Ritesh Shah (Writer), Ronnie Lahiri (Film producer), Sheel Kumar (Film producer) (16 October 2021). Sardar Udham (Motion Picture) (in Hindi and English). India: Rising Sun Films (Production company), Kino Works (Production company), Amazon Prime Video (Distributor). OCLC 1343155273
- "Ő is nálunk tanít: Gerevich András" [He also teaches with us: András Gerevich]. Budapest Metropolitan University (Interview) (in Hungarian). Interviewed by Budapest Metropolitan University. Budapest. 24 March 2020.
- Becker, Felicitas (18 February 2002). "Yugoslav war films: No Man's Land and Chico". Kinoeye. Vol. 2, no. 4.
- "Laptörténet" [Page history]. Jelenkor.net.
- József, Lapis (9 January 2015). "2014 KULTkölteményei (TOP 10)" [2014 KULT POEMS (TOP 10)]. Kulter.hu (in Hungarian).
- Schandl, Veronika (24 January 2020). "The Grande Dame: Magda Szabó – A Portrait". Hungarian Literature Online.
- Gömöri, George (2007-11-28). "Obituary: Magda Szabó". The Guardian. ISSN 0261-3077

- Hetzmann, Mercédesz (20 February 2022). "40-50% of Hungarian restaurants will fail and close". Daily News Hungary.
- Nehru part - English - WeloveBudapest". welovebudapest.com. 11 May 2021
- U.S. concerned over neo-Nazi groups after Hungarian rainbow flags torn down". August 17, 2020 – via Reuters. Reporting by Krisztina Fenyo; Writing by Krisztina Than; Editing by Alison Williams
- Christine E. Bose; Minjeong Kim, eds. (2009). Global Gender Research: Transnational Perspectives. Routledge. p. 198. ISBN 9781136083549.
- "Női szakasz: Zaklatás" [Women's Section: Harassment]. Magyar Narancs. Vol. 8, no. 29. Budapest: Magyarnarancs.hu Lapkiadó Kft. 18 July 1996
- Bridge, Adrian (20 July 1996). "Sex trade moguls thrive by the Blue Danube". The Independent.
- Feffer, John (April 28, 2014). "The Flowering of Feminism in Hungary". HuffPost.
- "A felfedezetlen kincs – a Közkincs Könyvtár bemutatkozik" [The undiscovered treasure - the Public Treasure Library presents itself]. juratus.elte.hu (in Hungarian). Eötvös Loránd University. 16 May 2019.
- Kessler, Gretchen (27 September 2019). "A visit to Budapest's unique, English-language feminist library". welovebudapest.com.
- Rita, Antoni (30 September 2019). "A prostitúció elválaszthatatlan a nők elleni erőszaktól" [Prostitution is inseparable from violence against women]. Nőkért.hu. A Nőkért Egyesület."The first panel was moderated by the founder of Közkincs Kiadó, veteran feminist activist Antonia Burrows (who at the time also contributed to the Feminist Network and was one of the founders of NANE)."
- "Közkincs Könyvtár." LMBT Történeti Hónap. Hungarian LGBT Alliance. 25 January 2020.
- Casimir-Favrot, Maïa (19 October 2020). "Manifestation de soutien aux #WomenInWhite : un appel à la solidarité féminine internationale" [Demonstration of support for #WomenInWhite: a call for international female solidarity]. Le Journal Francophone de Budapest (in French).
- "Kis magyar LMBTQ sajtótörténelem - A Hom-Erostól a Company-ig" [A little Hungarian LGBTQ press history - From Hom-Eros to Company]. Humen Online (in Hungarian). 1 January 2022.
- "History of the Department". das.elte.hu. ELTE School of English and American Studies. Retrieved 15 September 2023.

- @pride.for.sarah.hegazi (1 October 2023). "Today, October 1, is the birthday of #Sarah_Hegazi" – via Instagram.
- 'Egypt failed her': LGBT activist kills herself in Canada after suffering post-prison trauma". Middle East Eye. 15 June 2020.
- Randeria, Shalini (30 July 2022). "CEU Overjoyed to Finally See Justice for Our Student Ahmed Samir Santawy". ceu.edu. Central European University. "Statement by CEU President and Rector Shalini Randeria on the Exoneration of Our Student Ahmed Samir Santawy."
- "Aleppo" . Litera – az irodalmi portál (in Hungarian). Budapest: Litera.hu. 15 December 2016. "Jó ideje Aleppóról szólnak a hírek. A szíriai várost humanitárius katasztrófa fenyegeti, a négy éve dúló polgáháborúban több mint százezren estek áldozatul. Tegnap tűzszünetet hirdettek, ennek ellenére még mindig tart a vérfürdő. Ezt a verset a tragédiáról ma hajnalban érkezett szerkesztőségünkhöz". [Aleppo has been in the news for quite some time. The Syrian city is threatened by a humanitarian disaster, more than a hundred thousand people have fallen victim to the civil war that has been raging for four years. A ceasefire was announced yesterday, but the bloodbath is still going on. This poem about the tragedy arrived at our editorial office this morning.]
- George Miller (Writer, director, producer), Brendan McCarthy (Writer), Nico Lathouris (Writer), Byron Kennedy (Characters), PJ Voeten (Producer), PJ Voeten (Director) (7 May 2015). Mad Max: Fury Road (Motion Picture). Australia, USA: Village Roadshow Pictures (Production company), RatPac-Dune Entertainment (Production company), Kennedy Miller Mitchell (Production company), Roadshow Entertainment (Distributor), Warner Bros. Pictures (Distributor). OCLC 924712345
- Dávid, Kovács (14 September 2018). "Megérdemelte a Macskafogó a ráncfelvarrást" [The Cat Catcher deserved to be stitched up]. Index.hu (in Hungarian).
- BudaPost (19 October 2020)."Hungarian Press Roundup: Controversy over Promoting Gay Inclusion among Children". Hungary Today.
- Ursula von der Leyen (15 July 2021). "EU founding values: Commission starts legal action against Hungary and Poland for violations of fundamental rights of LGBTIQ people" (Press release). Brussels: European Commission.
- Kovács, Kinga; Garay, Annamária (18 July 2021). "Több a homofób támadás" [There are more homophobic attacks] (in Hungarian). RTL.hu

- Balu Mahendra (director) (8 July 1983). "Balu Mahendra's Sadma" [Trauma] (DVD) (in Hindi). Mumbai: Shemaroo Entertainment. OCLC 54097175.
- Magan, Srishti (3 December 2019). "Kamal Haasan Chasing Sridevi In Sadma's Climax Is The Most Heartbreaking Moment In Indian Cinema". ScoopWhoop. Archived from the original on 28 January 2023.
- "Letter to Uncle Sam by Saadat Hasan Manto". Wasafiri.org. August 12, 2017.
- "Dareechah-e-Nigaarish - Saadat Hasan Manto (1912-1955)". Dareechah.com. Retrieved 17 September 2023.
- "Mischief and Sorrow: An Interview with Jericho Brown". The Kenyon Review (Interview). Interviewed by Honorée Fanonne Jeffers. Gambier, Ohio: Kenyon College. July 2019. ISSN 0163-075X. JSTOR 0163075X
- "Inaugural". The New York Times Magazine. Illustration by Rob Sato. New York City, New York. January 20, 2021. "By Jericho Brown, winner of the 2020 Pulitzer Prize in Poetry, on the occasion of the inauguration of Joe Biden and Kamala Harris."
- Wamsley, Laurel (14 September 2023). "Seattle officer recorded joking about woman's death, saying 'she had limited value'". NPR.
- Sen, Sumanti (22 February 2024). "Who is Kevin Dave? All about Seattle cop who escaped charges after Jaahnavi Kandula's death". Hindustan Times.